Jasper

Jasper

MICHELLE GROCE

With Illustrations by Laura Duis

NOVELLO festival PRESS

Charlotte 2003

Library of Congress Cataloging-in-Publication Data

Groce, Michelle, 1960-
    Jasper / by Michelle Groce ; illustrated by Laura Duis.
        p. cm.
Summary: Jasper, a stray cat with the ability to sense impending danger,
must repeatedly decide whether to keep searching for the perfect home
for himself or to risk his own safety to protect others.
    ISBN 0-9708972-6-X
    [1. Cats--Fiction. 2. Owls--Fiction. 3. Psychic ability--Fiction.] I.
Duis, Laura, ill. II. Title.
    PZ7.G89235 Jas 2003
    [Fic]--dc21
                                        2002151748

Printed in China
FIRST EDITION

Book design by Leslie B. Rindoks

To the memory of my friends,
Wayne Kelly and Gilles Pelletier,

And my mother, who loved reading and cats
and had a soft spot for strays.

Chapter 1

E KNEW THE BOY WAS LEAVING. A wispy dream in a lazy day catnap turned vivid and real, like all the things he saw before they happened. The pictures came to him unbidden; he preferred to think of sunny days and bowls full of tuna fish, lovely red meat and hands that lived to scratch his chin. Much as he craved his thoughts of comfort and tried to hold them steady in his mind, they slipped away like smoke once the pictures started.

The boy was leaving and there was nothing he could do about it. The big truck would come and then the people in and out of the house, carrying things, always carrying them out. He could see the boy, eyes wide and dark, electric with fear, and the boy's mother, wiry and determined, in constant motion, shifting the little girl from one hip to the other. And the boy's father: tall and broad, talking on the phone, gesturing, pacing, speaking to the mother and the children without looking at them. Jasper could see it all and he shook his head and stretched and tried to think of something fun like grasshoppers, but the image of the boy, his face pale, kept interrupting. It was time to say good-bye.

Jasper opened his eyes and sat for a moment, sensing the day, feeling the insistent sun already hot on his fur. Home was an abandoned tree fort built by ambitious and resourceful children who had since outgrown the need for forts and clubs and secret blood oaths. It was reasonably dry, and in the temperate Carolina climate, reasonably warm. He was an optimistic cat and still believed that one day he would find a home, a real home, with regular meals and a warm place to sleep every night.

The truth was that Jasper didn't have the kind of looks that softened the hearts of humans. He groomed himself as well as he could but his coat was on the splotchy side, one ear had been notched in an unfortunate encounter with a Chow, and his right back leg had taken a twist in a separate incident with a Chevy Malibu.

He trotted with purpose through the woods and across the back yards toward the boy's house. At the edge of the big angry man's yard, next door to the boy, the cat crouched down and scanned for any sign of the owner. He lifted his head and tasted deeply of the air. All clear. The big man's back yard was the fastest way to the boy's window even if the man did hate the sight of all cats, especially Jasper. But then, Jasper thought, there wasn't much the big man seemed to like.

A dozen running strides and he was across the danger zone, into the target back yard and heading straight for the boy's bedroom window. The window was open a few inches, the boy's signal to come inside, but before Jasper scrambled up the tree and into the room, he crept around toward the front. No sign of the truck yet. He sighed with relief and scaled the tree. From the window ledge, he could see the boy sitting on his bed, which had been stripped of all sheets and blankets. Boxes were stacked all around the room and the walls were bare, dotted with pinholes and one or two nails. The boy was leafing through a comic book, but even from the window, Jasper could see the boy's eyes were dull and unseeing; he turned the pages far too quickly to absorb them.

A quick leap to the window ledge and then a flattening under the glass, pushing the screen open with his nose, and Jasper was inside. From the window to the boy's lap took two quick bounds and then the boy's arms were tight around him.

"Oh, Jasper," he said. "I was so afraid you wouldn't come." He hugged the cat too closely. Jasper squeaked softly, politely for the boy to lighten up, but he could feel the boy's heart beating like the wings of a moth and the wetness that splashed on his head and his back was like something precious so he closed his eyes until the boy loosened his grip.

Finally the boy pulled away enough so that he could look the cat full in the face. The boy's face was pale, just like Jasper had seen it in his mind pictures. "I wish I could take you with me," the boy said.

Jasper told the boy that he understood and that he loved him the only way he knew: a long slow blink and purring with his whole body.

For the last year, the boy had fed Jasper with cat food he bought with his own money despite the disapproval of his parents. The mother had taken one look at the cat and shook her head, pulling her toddler daughter close as if Jasper carried some contagion.

He always met the boy at the bus stop in the morning and the afternoon, with gifts if he could manage it, of frogs and field mice and once a tiny wren. All of his gifts were live: the highest form of cat favor, to share the pleasure of the hunt with another. Truth told, Jasper wasn't too keen on the kill. He much preferred the pungent moist lumpiness of canned cat food to the messy irregularity of his own hunting efforts.

There was a quick movement at the corner of his eye and then he heard her, "Kitty, kitty. Want to pet the kitty."

It was the boy's sister, three years of strident, grabby energy concentrated in one small, quick person. Her face bright, hands outstretched, fingers splayed, she bore down on Jasper like a drunken bee. He tensed and waited for the hair-pulling, skin-twisting pain that was her version of "pet the kitty." Usually he tried to avoid the child but today was moving day and he would not leave the boy until he absolutely had to.

"No!" the boy said, and stuck out his leg to block the toddler's progress.

The child looked at Jasper, then at her brother, then back to Jasper. Her mouth opened so he could see the tiny white squares that were her front teeth and the bubble-gum pink of her tongue. The scream was a healthy one, full of anger and frustration.

The mother's face appeared at the door. "Edward! Have you let that mangy cat in again? Outside! Now! I don't have time for this!"

Edward was the name she called the boy when she was angry. The little girl continued to wail. The mother continued to shout. Jasper gave the boy's hand two quick strokes with his tongue, just to let him know he'd be waiting, then he leaped to the window and was outside.

The long jointed truck was angling into the driveway of the big angry man, who stood on his front sidewalk, fists on his hips, head forward. Jasper slipped into the front shrubbery to watch.

"What the Sam Hill do you think you're doing?" The big man's face was red and inflamed, as usual, below razor-parted hair that waved just so over his brow. He wore crisp khakis, belted below his big, hard belly. Jasper licked his paws reflectively and thought of how the man resembled a turtle, only instead of carrying his shell on his back, the big man carried it in front.

The truck shuddered to a halt and the driver's door opened with a heavy metallic squawk. A lanky man with a clipboard in his hand hopped out and started across the manicured lawn toward the big man.

"Stop!" The man thrust out a meaty arm, palm flat, sausage fingers extended.

"'Scuse me?" The driver stopped walking.

"You take one more step on my lawn, I'll have you in court on trespassing charges."

The driver looked down at the impeccable carpet of green, then back up at the big man. "Well, I am sorry about touching your lawn and all, but in the interest of moving you and your family, I have to tell you, it might not be the last time it happens today."

The air around the big man fairly quivered with rage. "That's what I'm trying to tell you, dummy. You're not moving me anywhere. You're at the wrong house." He jerked a forefinger in Jasper's direction. "They're moving, not me."

The driver stared at the big man. "Well, why didn't you just say so?"

When the big man cursed and took a few steps toward the driver and another man got out of the truck, a massive square man with biceps like hams and no expression on his face, Jasper knew it was time to step in. He didn't like the big man but it didn't take any psychic ability to see that this could turn ugly and there was something about ugliness that turned Jasper's stomach hollow.

Jasper trotted onto the big man's lawn, appreciating the fine thick texture of the grass. He strolled over close enough to the men to feel the disturbance in the air while keeping a careful eye on the big feet. It was in moods like this that men were prone to boot a cat senseless.

He headed for a large precise circle of a planting bed directly in the big man's line of vision. A series of spidery young dogwoods grew in a semicircle, surrounded at exact intervals by impatiens alternating red and white, purple and white. Jasper snaked through the impatiens, into a tight curve around the tree, and then stopped as if to scent the air. He cut his eyes back at the big man to see if he'd been noticed.

Yes indeed, the big man had stepped on his own precious lawn, to the left of the two moving men, so that he could keep a watchful eye on the cat. Jasper smiled a secret cat smile and began to scratch like he needed to make a deposit.

"NO!" The big man hustled toward the planting bed, leaving the moving men mid-sentence. Jasper let the big man get two or three steps away, close enough to smell the astringent, heavy smell of him, when he bounded over to the next tree and gave a few quick scratches. The big man followed like the ex-linebacker he was and again, Jasper gauged his distance. The moving men were watching, talking to each other, and then as Jasper had hoped, the boy's father came out of his front door.

"Hey! What are you fellows doing over there? I'm the one that's moving."

The movers shook their heads and waved and headed back to the truck. While Jasper watched the other men, the big man had gotten too close and when he grabbed for the cat, his hand rested on Jasper's back for a second, like a hot grasping vise. Jasper flattened himself and bounded back over to the boy's yard while the big man growled and muttered.

He moved back into the shrubbery at the front of the boy's house, where he had a good view of the articulated truck edging back down the correct driveway. When the truck stopped, followed by a series of heavy hollow thuds and slams and the rumbling of men's voices, Jasper watched closely as the back of the unit opened into a long shadowed cave. Surely there were plenty of places for one skinny cat to hide in such a cavern. He waited for the men to trudge into the house then crept up the slanted ramp to peer into the opening.

It was a long, tall empty box with the most confusing array of ghostly smells he'd ever inhaled. Like all cats, he knew that every human had a trademark aroma, distinctive as a fingerprint. People who lived together developed a family scent. Anything that people brought into their home took on that odor: furniture, books, clothing and even the pets. This steel box smelled like wisps and remnants and shadows of dozens of families, multi-layered and intoxicating. So many stories in the smells.

He blinked and took a few tentative steps inside, his nose to the steel floor. Dimly, he heard the low rumble of the men's voices and heavy footsteps approaching, but his nose was twitching hard and he just couldn't pull away from those fascinating faint perfumes. A series of thumps shook the van, and he turned to the opening to see the two moving men guiding a hand truck with a washing machine straight at him. He darted around them and leaped from the edge, ignoring the ramp.

Safe inside the front shrubbery, Jasper sat and watched and strained to hear something that would give him some clue as to where the boy was moving. The two men didn't talk much beyond the occasional shorthand exchange. Trip after trip, they moved quickly, efficiently, their hand trucks stacked with boxes. The repetition made Jasper sleepy, and so he dozed in the filtered fingers of sun that stretched through the shrubs. He started to give himself a bath but his heart wasn't in it. There was a dull ache in his gut and for once, it had nothing to do with hunger.

It wasn't long before the men were sliding the ramp back into the sleeve under the opening and slamming shut the panel to the packed truck cave. The father came outside and spoke to the men before the truck lumbered out of the driveway and down the street. The front door banged as he went back inside and the boy came out and stood on the front porch, calling Jasper's name in a hoarse, urgent whisper.

Jasper leaned against the boy's legs and blinked up at him. The boy squatted and set down a paper plate heaped with canned cat food. Jasper dug in.

"This is for you, buddy." Not that he'd needed the clarification. The boy sat on the lowest front step and watched, rubbing his eyes and petting the cat with long sweeping strokes. Jasper ate until his belly was stretched tight then sat down to bathe. The boy hugged him close again and the smell of the boy, a pleasing mix of oiled baseball glove and fresh grass and Cheerios, was all Jasper could smell and he thought this must be like heaven, a full belly and unabashed love, except without the moving van. The boy studied Jasper's face like he wanted to burn the image in his brain.

"I tried to find somebody to take care of you, Jasper," the boy was saying. "But people want kittens. They won't even come look at a grown cat." He shook his head. "And now, my dad says —" he tried to continue but his eyes were spilling again. The hand stroking Jasper had become sweaty and heavy.

Jasper started to squirm.

"My dad says that we have to take you to the animal shelter." The boy's eyes were dark and soft and begging for forgiveness but Jasper heard footsteps approaching the front door from inside. He pulled away from the boy. The boy's arms tightened but it's hard to hold a cat with other ideas. And Jasper had the distinct idea that he'd had enough of good-byes. He'd certainly had enough of animal shelters on that first trip, two years previous, the first time he'd ever had the mind pictures.

He'd been dozing in his own wire cage when the images came to him. The cat, a scruffy orange female with a foul temper, was crouched on a steel table in the back room. She'd growled, a rusty chainsaw of a growl, and he'd seen the gloved hands holding her down. Another hand picked up a fold of skin, then a hovering needle jabbed. The cat spat and hissed. She quivered a little, her head rolled, and then she sank down like she was melting inside. She didn't move again. Jasper had wakened, shaking with fear, dreading every pair of hands that came toward him. He'd thought it was a nightmare until he looked around for the ill-tempered orange cat.

Jasper had gotten to the middle of the front yard when he heard the father's voice.

"Well, Eddie, go ahead and get him. We don't have all day."

The boy turned toward Jasper and squatted down, one hand outstretched. "Jasper?"

The cat stopped and looked back at the boy. No, there would be no more animal shelter for him if he could help it. Not even for a few more minutes with the boy, gambling on the slim chance that the parents might wake up to the horror of what they suggested. The father carried a box of houseplants to the car. The mother had a big canvas tote over her shoulder and a small cooler in one hand. With the other hand, she gestured to the little girl, who skipped and hopped around the boy.

"Hey, Eddie, whatcha doing?"

"Go away, Megan." The boy ignored her and kept his eyes fixed on Jasper's.

"Come on, Megan. Hurry up, Eddie." The mother followed the father out to the car and the little girl trailed behind.

Jasper watched the boy and his family and wondered again, as he often did, what it would be like to be a part of something like that tiny tribe.

"Jasper boy? Are you going to come with me or do you have someplace else to go? Are you going to be all right?" The boy whispered now and picked at a scab on his arm. He seemed to be talking more to himself than Jasper.

With two quick silent bounds, Jasper was close enough to touch the boy. So he did, stepping close in a tight circle around him so that he gave the boy a full body brush. The boy's head jerked up and his hand reached out, but the specter of the shelter loomed cold and deadly in Jasper's mind so he stepped outside the boy's range.

"Eddie, are you coming?" The father stood beside the car, both hands on his hips.

"Jasper?" the boy asked. Jasper trotted a few yards away then blinked a long slow caress to his boy.

The little girl spoke up in her thin, reedy voice, "Why is Eddie crying?"

Jasper didn't need to hear the answer and the thought of watching the car pull out of the driveway and out of his life was suddenly too much to ask. He took off in a loping, uneven gallop across the big man's yard without stopping to look back.

Chapter 2

HE MOON WAS SWOLLEN AND FULL and Jasper was relieved. It was on such nights that the moon was the most outgoing, the most likely to talk freely and sweetly and smile down on him with a warmth that made him feel like a kitten again, nestled at the belly of a loving, generous mother.

He'd found a good spot on top of the tree fort that he called home and there he stretched, waiting for the moon to rise above the tree line. The boy's leaving had made the ache in his gut more tender; with each breath he could feel it, a knot that reminded him of the time he'd happened upon the picnic in the park with the unattended tub of potato salad. He'd eaten like a starving thing; at the time he'd been hungry too many days running. Then the people returned, accompanied by a Schnauzer, who was, of course, indignant and energetic and chased him for several hundred yards. That's when he got the pain. Jasper sighed. Why did his life have to be this way? Why were scraps and stolen bits all he ever got?

"The boy gave you more than scraps." It was the moon, in her rich low voice, responding to his thoughts.

It was true, he knew. The boy had given him his best. Why did it have to end?

The moon didn't answer. Ripe and inscrutable, she balanced in the night sky like an open-ended promise.

So the problem was with him. He wanted too much, expected too much. He was a mangy, ragged stray cat who needed to learn gratitude for anything tossed his way.

"It wouldn't hurt," she said, "and it also wouldn't hurt to lose the self-pity."

"You expect too much of me," Jasper cried out in frustration. "I'm a cat, remember? A simple, self-indulgent feline. We're not known for character, you understand."

The moon just smiled.

"Cats are known for grace and style and independence." He shook his head. "Not exactly strengths of mine. I'm just your average cat and I want a place to settle down. Is that asking too much?"

A thin spotty cloud passed over the face of the moon. He waited. The cloud thickened into a veil that might have been anger. He'd not asked such hard questions before. He'd not had reason. He stared into the implacable black sky and squinted at the hard little lights of the stars.

His gut ached dully while he considered his options. He could try to track the boy down in his new home. He'd heard stories of cats doing it but he didn't have any confidence in his own ability to track the boy all the streets and yards away that his parents had surely taken him. His experiences with the animal shelter, subsequent escape, and home hunting after that had convinced him that the world was a big, mostly uncaring place. One did better to pick a small territory and learn it well.

He could stick primarily to the woods and make his own living without humans, which meant hunting his own food, water, and shelter. Uck. Again, he'd heard the stories but he just couldn't see himself doing it unless he had no other options.

The last option was to shadow the neighborhood and see if anybody would take pity on a poor abandoned cat. There was that woman with the frosty hair and the red fingernails who had spoken kindly to him a few times. He'd seen the Persian in her bay window. Jasper had picked up lip-reading in his time in the neighborhood and the things the Persian cat said when she spotted him outside the window were rude and distinctly unfriendly. He would have to try it anyway.

"That's the spirit." The moon's voice caught him by surprise and the sweetness of it soothed the ache in his belly. He looked up and gave the moon one of his long, luscious eye kisses before he curled himself into his sleep knot.

Chapter 3

NUMBER OF DAYS PASSED before Jasper got hungry enough to take a trot by the home of the frosty-haired woman. Luck was with him and she was out front, on her knees in the flowerbed by her mailbox. She glanced up as Jasper approached.

"Hello there, handsome." The woman smelled of bug repellant and cigarettes. She wore heavy gardening gloves and a straw hat with two ragged daisies in the brim. An assortment of gardening tools and a scramble of pulled weeds were piled beside her.

Jasper sat a respectable two feet away.

The woman stopped her digging and studied him. "You belonged to that little boy who lived down the street, didn't you? Don't tell me they up and moved without you."

He blinked at her, flirting, and meowed.

She pulled off a glove and stretched a hand out toward him.

He sniffed her fingers politely and rubbed his head against them. The woman knew exactly what human fingernails had been designed to do. What bliss. He leaned luxuriously into the pressure.

"I can't believe they'd leave a sweet boy like you behind. Who's taking care of you now?" She peered into his face like she expected a response.

He shifted his body so that she could reach that exquisite place at the top of his tail. The woman cooed and scratched his back, between his ears, under his chin, and he closed his eyes with the sheer, oozing pleasure of it all. He sprawled on his back in the grass while she gently rubbed his belly.

Finally she pulled her gloves on and kneeled back down in the planting bed. Jasper dozed, loving the companionable heat of the sun, the tantalizing summer air, and the sense of the woman nearby. Life could be lovely, even for a scruffy stray.

Then he smelled it: the faint rank odor of dog. Big, hostile dog, to be exact. The smell was wafting, curling around him like smoke from an invisible fire. He kept catching little whiffs of dog and given the unseasonably light and playful nature of the breeze that day, the beast could be one yard or several away.

He stood, reluctantly, and lifted his nose to taste deeply of the air. He heard it before he saw it. The rasp of toenails on asphalt, the muffled jingle of a choke collar, and then the smell of it was strong enough to make his mouth run dry. The dog was a heavy-headed mutt, muscular and springy, moving purposefully, head low between his shoulders, scanning the street and yards as if he had business in the vicinity and couldn't remember the exact address.

Jasper looked around for the closest tree, a mid-sized maple and began to edge toward it, keeping his eyes on the dog. The mutt slowed in front of the woman, who picked up her shovel and stood. She shaded her eyes with one hand and watched the dog, which sniffed vaguely in her direction and then continued down the street.

Jasper and the woman watched the dog to be sure he was well on his anvil-headed way. Satisfied, he eased back to his spot in the sun, warmer now than when he'd left it. The woman set the shovel down and dropped slowly back to her knees.

He had closed his eyes and tasted the ripe summer air again, feeling the friendly hot hand of the sun stroking him like another kind soul when he felt the thumping tremors through the ground. He tensed and leaped for the tree, praying the dog hadn't gotten too good a start on him. The smell of dog was so strong in his nose and throat that he nearly choked but the tree was only a few short jumps away. He thought he felt the hot, sour breath of the beast on his tail but he wouldn't risk the split second of forward momentum it would cost him to look. The woman shouted at the dog, which was murderously silent. It all happened in an instant, but the seconds flattened and stretched and roared in his ears like a ruthless river.

One last push and he was scrambling up the tree, digging with his claws, praying for traction. The dog jumped, leaning his front paws on the trunk, and began to bark and curse and taunt Jasper to come down and fight.

"Hey, hairball!" the dog said. "Come on down and join the party."

"Hey, Fido," Jasper said. "Go drink some pond scum." Dogs hated to be called Fido.

The dog snarled. "What's that supposed to mean? Coward! Pipsqueak! Rat with a tail!"

"Hey fathead," Jasper said. "Keep it down. Can't you see this is a peaceful neighborhood? At least it used to be, before you showed up."

The dog stopped barking and drew his lips back in a vicious smile. The blast from the garden hose caught him unawares and he whimpered with the cold wet shock of it. Tail curled back between his legs, he tried to approach the woman.

She kept the hose directed on him. "Get out of my yard, dog. Get out before I call the pound on you." She brandished the shovel and stomped at him. "Don't think I won't do it. Git!"

With great satisfaction, Jasper watched him slink out of the yard and lope away. He watched for a long time, until the beast was well out of sight and the smell of dog and Jasper's own queasy fear had left the air.

The woman stood, hands on her hips, garden hose still in her grip, shaking her head. "Folks just let their dogs run wild. What do you expect?" She pulled a pack of cigarettes out of one baggy pocket and lit one. The smell of it was acrid and harsh, yet comforting.

A picture flashed through Jasper's mind of a figure lying in bed, propped on pillows facing a humming television broadcasting mottled gray snow. Smoke was filling the room. A sputtering fan on top of a pile of magazines sparked encouragement to a small, growing dance of flames.

A shudder passed through him. He picked his way down out of the tree and rubbed against the woman's legs with real affection. He had to figure out some way to spend the night inside or else make sure the Persian understood. He looked up at the woman and meowed his thanks for the rescue.

"You are a sweet boy, aren't you?" She bent down and scratched his head. "I'll bet you're hungry. How long has it been since you've eaten? Look at how skinny you are."

He followed her around to the back door and waited patiently on the brick patio. The yard was nice – lots of bushes and flowers, meaning butterflies and birds. He wasn't much of a hunter but he did love to sit in the sun and watch the colors flash through slitted eyes and fantasize his swift, stealthy attack.

A petulant feline face appeared at the screen door. She saw Jasper and started to growl. "Get out of my yard."

He jumped up and approached her. "Hi! Please don't be upset. I'm not trying to steal your person. There's something I need to tell you. Something important."

She snarled and spit, "How could a bum like you have anything important to tell me?"

"It's about the way she falls asleep on the bed watching television."

The white cat spasmed into a hissing, spitting rage. "You've been spying! You sleazy, low-life excuse for a cat. I'll kill you!"

"Precious!" the woman said. "Good heavens! Calm down, child."

Precious paid no attention. "I'll rip you to shreds. Shreds! You're an ugly bum. You don't belong here. You're a loser. Go find a garbage can. I have a pedigree. This is my place. My person! Get it?"

"You have to listen to me," Jasper tried again.

"I don't have to do anything you say, loser! What I have to do is get your mangy stray carcass out of my yard!"

Jasper sighed and lay down with his back to Precious and tried to ignore her. He liked it better when he could only see her through the window. Her voice was harsh and penetrating. The truth in what she said stung. He'd had more meals from garbage cans and trash heaps than canned cat food. He'd be willing to bet that Precious had her very own food and water bowls. He wished he had the strength of character to slip away before the woman reappeared with the food but he'd been hungry for too many days.

"Here's a little something for the boy." The woman had come back outside, maneuvering around the still-volatile Precious. Precious lunged for the door but the woman was too quick for her.

The wonderful woman placed two plastic bowls in front of him — one filled with cool fresh water and one heaped with lovely pungent canned food. He sniffed at the food, whiskers quivering, tingling with anticipation, and began to eat in great grasping mouthfuls.

"Whoa there, handsome." The woman was watching him. "Slow down or you'll choke yourself."

He heard her but he couldn't help himself. In a matter of minutes, he had finished the bowl and was rubbing against her legs in abject devotion and love and hope for more.

"That's all for now, sweetie. Don't want you to make yourself sick."

And so the afternoon passed with Jasper pleasantly fogged by the effect of a full, rich meal, dozing by the back door until the woman came outside to finish her gardening. He followed her around the front of the house and settled in the grass a dozen feet away from the planting bed. He tried to think of how he was going to sneak inside so that he could stand guard against sparking fans and late night television but the problem was a massive flat wall in his mind and he was far too relaxed to consider the options properly. He would think of something.

Afternoon stretched into dusk and before long the light had softened and the fireflies were beginning their slow deliberate blinks. Normally they were a comfort to Jasper, the blinking a personal coded message of reassurance for him that all would be well. But the intoxication of the rich meal had waned and he could feel the weight of the premonition like an extra layer of fur. He scanned the evening sky for the moon and the sky stared back, streaky, shadowed, and faceless.

The frosty-haired woman had finished rolling up the garden hose and storing her tools. She sat heavily on the back steps and began taking off her shoes. He rubbed against her legs, caressing with his tail.

"What are we going to do with you, Mr. Friendly?" She scratched him under the chin. "You're not much to look at but you're just a big sweetheart, aren't you?"

He ducked his head into the shoes she had just taken off and rubbed luxuriously, as if the woman's feet smelled like heaven on earth. "I'd bring you inside but I know Precious would have a fit and fall in it."

He licked her hand, just a little, to let her know he was willing to take his chances with Precious. She gave his head a final rub and stood. "You have a good evening, Mr. Friendly Fred. Maybe we'll see you later."

When the door closed behind her and Precious' contorted face showed up in the kitchen window, Jasper trotted around to the side of the house. Lucky for him, it was one story, so he wouldn't need any opportune trees or fancy climbing and jumping. He needed to figure out which windows opened into the woman's bedroom. The house was dark except for the kitchen, so he continued to circle around front, looking for trees close enough to the house to give him access. That's when he heard the jingle.

A split second later, he smelled the mutt and someone else, and when he saw the dog, his worst fears were confirmed. The dog with the blunt and brutal head was trotting down the street, his choke collar attached to a leash held by the big angry man. When had this happened? The big angry man had no pets. Pets soiled a yard and made noise and dug up hours of hard work. What was the big angry man doing with a dog?

The dog had caught the cat's scent and strained against the leash, wheezing for breath. The big man peered into the yard. Jasper flattened himself in the grass, hoping he would blend into the shadows, but the big man's eyes were sharp.

"There he is, boy." He leaned over and unsnapped the leash. "Get him."

The only thing that saved him was the dog's bad eyesight. Freed of the leash, he hurtled across the yard without barking. Jasper had started for the tree and the dog overran himself. He wheeled and lunged after Jasper, snapping the air behind him. One of the snaps clamped down on Jasper's tail. He screamed in pain and fury and raked at the dog's left eye. The dog dropped his hold on Jasper's tail and lunged for his neck. Jasper sidestepped the attack and leaped for the tree, his tail feeling like it was on fire.

Up he scrambled, until he sat gasping on a limb, trembling and shaking, his mouth dry as dust. The dog started his barking and cursing. The big man laughed as he stomped across the yard, stopping beside his protégé.

"Good job, Max." He thumped the dog's body a few times but the dog's attention was still focused on Jasper.

"That was close, scumbag. Your tail tastes good. I can't wait to see what the rest of you tastes like," the dog shouted with pleasure.

Jasper didn't respond. Plenty of

dogs had chased him, but none were so focused and hateful as this beast. The fear worked dreadful cold fingers down into his bones and wrapped around his heart like a treacherous friend. He concentrated on holding on to the tree and not looking at his tail just yet.

The front door slammed.

"What's going on out here?" The frosty-haired woman stood on her front porch, hands on her hips.

"Oh, nothing to get worked up about. Max's just having a little chase with a stray cat that's been bothering the whole neighborhood." The man smiled at the dog like a co-conspirator and gestured up toward Jasper. "Didn't hurt him."

"I'll thank you to leave my yard now, Mr. Peeler." The woman's voice was hard-edged as a hoe. "If I find your dog running loose again, I'll be calling the pound."

"Hey now, don't get all mad. Max wasn't going to hurt the cat." The big man's face was red, as usual. An image flashed though Jasper's mind: the sleeping figure he had seen earlier, but a closer view. And it dawned on him that the body in the bed before the humming television and the small flames wasn't the woman at all. It was the big angry man. The thought washed over him like a warm and fragrant breeze and he stopped shaking.

He looked at the big man, now snapping the leash back on the snarling dog's collar and he could see the man's mouth open and his face grow a deeper, brighter red but Jasper wasn't listening anymore. The cat was adrift with relief and a certain deep satisfaction that the big man and the vicious dog were surely going to get what was coming to them. It was only fair. Nasty, unpleasant beings deserved punishment, didn't they? And in his experience, they didn't get punished nearly often or adequately enough.

And yet something else was nagging at him. He could picture the wise, knowing face of the moon as she would look at him in this situation. He glanced at the sky and sure enough, the thin curve of her luminous face hung heavy on the edge of the sky. She didn't say a word, just looked at him, deep at him, as if she could see into him.

Without a word, he knew she understood how perfect it would be for him if the big angry man and the heavy-headed dog were to disappear out of his life. What did she expect him to do? Try to sneak inside the big angry man's house?

"Kitty? Friendly Freddie? Sweet boy?" The woman stood at the base of the tree, her face turned up toward him like an aging flower. "Are you all right?"

The man and the dog were out of sight. Jasper's tail throbbed. He sighed and started down the tree, slowly, painfully. When he got to the bottom, he had to stop and rest.

"What happened to your tail, baby? That big ugly creep got ahold of you, didn't he?" He let the woman have a closer look but he avoided her hands when she tried to pick him up. The last thing he felt like right now was listening to the harangues of dear Precious and if the woman did take him inside, he'd never get back out in time.

In time for what, he wondered.

"You know," the moon replied.

He moved slowly through the neighborhood toward the abandoned fort that was more his home than any other place. He could hear the woman calling him the whole way but there were times a cat had to be alone and this was clearly one of them.

Chapter 4

Y THE TIME HE REACHED THE FORT, he felt exhausted and achy and all he wanted was to curl up and tend to his tail before he fell asleep. He picked a tight, inside perch, between the uneven roof and the smooth cleft in two thick branches, where he wouldn't have to deal with the moon. It worked for a while. His tail was sore and tacky with blood. By the time he had it licked clean, he knew that nothing was broken, just some deep bruising punctures that would eventually heal.

He slept until a hoot owl landed on top of the fort and began calling. Surely the owl would leave shortly. He tried to close his eyes and drift back to the sweet fog of sleep but the owl continued his repetitive, hollow hooting. Finally, Jasper sighed and stretched and climbed out of his safe little nook to address the situation.

"Excuse me," Jasper said, poking his head up just enough to see the stocky mottled back of the owl. He was a big one, probably as tall as Jasper would be if he stood on his hind legs.

The owl ignored him. Or possibly didn't hear him.

"Excuse me," he said more loudly. The owl twisted his neck

completely around in that eerie owl way and fixed Jasper with his big yellow eyes.

"Would you mind finding another place to have your evening? I've had a rough day and I really need the rest."

The owl rocked from side to side, repositioning to face him squarely. Settled, he gave a long, slow blink. He was nearly the size of the boy's young sister. The thought of the boy hit a tender place and just like that, Jasper lost his patience.

"Go away! This is my place!"

The owl looked at him.

Jasper snarled and began to flick his tail until it throbbed. He was tired of getting pushed around. The bird was big but he was, after all, just a bird.

"Just a bird," the owl echoed.

The chill moved down Jasper's back like a quivering little worm. "What did you say?" Jasper crouched down low on his haunches.

"Did I stutter? I'm not in the habit of stuttering." The owl puffed up his chest a little.

Fat, pompous fool, thought Jasper.

"There's nothing fat about me," the owl said. "It's my build. All muscle, just like my mom."

"How do you do that?" Jasper said, irritated but intrigued.

The owl puffed a bit larger. "Well, I get a lot of exercise and I'm really careful about what I eat—"

"I'm not talking about your build," Jasper interrupted. "How do you know what I'm thinking?"

"Oh," the owl said, visibly deflated.

He tried to soften it. "I mean, obviously, you're in great shape, but to know what others are thinking, that's really something."

"Really?" The owl cocked his head, stood a little straighter.

"Sure!" He studied the stout bird. "Doesn't it seem that way to you?"

The owl shrugged. "I suppose. It's not something I can control.

When I'd most like to be able to do it, to make the hunt easier, it's impossible. It's not like it's ever done me or anybody else a lot of good."

"How about humans?"

The owl blinked. "Humans? I don't spend enough time around them to know."

"Dogs?" Jasper asked.

"Don't know any dogs. You're my first cat. Cats are usually scared of me. I spend a lot of time by myself." The owl cocked his head and looked up at the evening sky.

The chill moved along Jasper's spine again. He had to look up, too.

The moon was a slim gleaming crescent.

"I wish she wouldn't do that," the owl said.

"Do what?" said Jasper.

"Turn away like that. I always think she's got another life with another world that we know nothing about, and when she shrinks like that, she's with them." The owl scratched the roof of the fort with one horny talon.

"I never thought of it that way." Jasper peered into the night sky and tried to imagine another world on the other side of the moon where hearts and eyes looked to her for comfort and guidance and her peculiar gifts. Even the idea of others on this side of the moon was staggering – the owl, for example. His head began to ache with the possibilities. Then the image of the bedside fire came back to him, so strong he smelled smoke and he had a sudden wrenching feeling he might be too late.

"Heaven forbid!" The owl stared at him with huge astonished eyes. "What's that all about?"

Jasper shook his head. The awful grinding weight of his fear flooded back into his gut. Fear of the big angry man and the vicious dog. The conflicting, cavernous fear of doing nothing.

"I've got to go." Jasper said, trotting to the edge of the roof to hide the shaking he could feel jerking through his limbs like inner thunder.

"I'll come too," the owl said and stretched out his wings.

Jasper looked sharply at the owl. "What's your name?"

The owl thought for a minute. "My brother used to call me Hank."

"Well, Hank, I'm Jasper. Stay here." He leaped from the fort to the ground and instantly regretted it. His bad back leg felt stiff and unresponsive and his tail ached; he willed himself to begin a fast trot without limping. He heard the soft whoosh of wings behind him.

He tried to think of what would happen in the big angry man's yard. Would the heavy-headed dog be running loose? He felt a jagged hollow feeling in the bottom of his stomach, like he'd swallowed something wrong. Wary of Hank close by, he tried to make his mind a smooth, dark blank but a seed of thought had sprouted. Why not find some other place, hidden away from the watchful eye of the moon and the intrusive owl and just forget it?

All the images he'd ever had were of events already in play. He'd never had the chance to try to change an outcome. Survival—that's what the images had done for him: escaping the animal shelter, scavenging a meal here and there, saying goodbye to the boy.

I'm just a cat. A selfish shabby stray cat.

What was this pull? This suffocating sense of dread at the thought of hiding away for the night? It didn't make a bit of sense. Here he was, more run-down and beat-up than ever before and less inclined to help the two in need than any two strangers. So why did it feel so wrong to do nothing to help them?

Jasper was pacing through the neighborhood, not thinking much about where he was going when he looked up and saw he was in the boy's old yard, under a willow oak with low, sturdy branches. Next door, the angry man's house was dark and quiet except for the play of light in a back window.

Fear squeezed his heart like a malicious fist. He could feel the shaking again and his mouth went dry. He took a deep breath, tasting the air for any hint of dog or fire. He heard a faint, dim whoosh that might have been the panting of a dog. He scrambled up the trunk of the willow oak. The breeze ruffled the leaves of the oak and the dog did not appear. Fear hummed in him, told him he had done his part; he had come and checked and found no fire to speak of, so he could move on with a clear conscience to someplace safe.

"Really?" Hank's voice came from the darkness of the limb just beyond him.

Jasper jerked and nearly fell out of the tree. He hissed in rage and fright.

"Sorry," said Hank.

"You should be," said Jasper. "What are you doing, sneaking up on me like that?"

"I thought I might be able to help."

"I don't need any help. I don't want you here. I told you that." Jasper looked at Hank with his most predatory stare.

Hank just looked back at him with enormous round eyes and Jasper had the oddest sensation, as if Hank's eyes were the reverse image of the moon.

"It's not easy, is it?" Hank said. "I mean I'm not a pack animal either. I don't know what I'm doing any more than you do. But here we are and there's the house, right? The one you were thinking about?" He nodded toward the flickering window. "Tell you what, I'll go take a closer look and see what I can see."

He lifted his wings before Jasper could answer and with a muffled whirring, flew straight toward the windowsill of the big man's bedroom. The sill was a narrow brick ledge and he could see it was no easy landing for stocky Hank but the owl settled on it, light as ash.

The sound of the dog's barking was frenzied, deeply vicious, and Jasper could feel the involuntary shaking deep in his bones. Hank didn't move, fixed on the ledge, peering in the window like an investigating officer.

The big man was shouting. Hoarse, deep shouts with no clear words. The dog's voice and the man's voice mingled in confusion, and fear gave Jasper a curious calm. *What were they getting so upset about?*

It was only an owl perched on the windowsill. Hank stuck there; steady as a star, and Jasper felt a push of respect for the stocky bird. Then the creaking sound of protesting wood – the big man was trying to open the window and only then did Hank lift his wings and start pumping.

But then if I could take off and fly anytime I wanted, I'd be a lot less afraid. That would be the thing. If I could fly.

"I can fly but you move a lot quicker on the ground." Hank settled next to him on the branch, ghostly quiet and startling. He glanced over at Jasper's feet. "You've got great claws."

"Well, what about those talons?"

"They're not bad. It's just, for close fights, you can't beat the claws. On the ground…" Hank shrugged.

"But you've got the beak!" Jasper said, eyeing the curved and pointed cruelty of it. "Surely that would be a big help."

Hank cocked his head. "It is, so long as you're dealing with something that doesn't have a mouth big enough to bite your whole head."

"Well, of course," Jasper said and shuddered at the thought.

The back door to the big man's house opened and they stopped talking. The big angry man stood there in boxer shorts and a white tee shirt stretched tight over his considerable belly. He peered into the night and swayed. Mumbling to himself, he squatted unsteadily to pick up a handful of rocks.

The dog pushed past him and burst into the yard, wild with excitement and anger. He rushed along the brick wall to the point underneath the bedroom window where Hank had been. He sniffed up great gulps of air, then stood trembling, straining to hear clues in the night.

Great, thought Jasper. *Just terrific.*

"At least they're not in the bedroom," Hank said, and his voice seemed to ring out into the night like a renegade bell.

"Sssh," Jasper told him but it was too late. The dog had heard. He bounded toward them, sniffing and straining. Jasper willed his heart to slow, his breathing to stay steady and calm, but he could feel his mouth drying up like a parched petal, his coat beginning to shed. The dog moved underneath the tree where they sat and watched.

"We need to tell you something," Hank said clearly to the heavy-headed dog. Jasper thought his heart would pound through his chest.

"Shut up," he hissed fiercely at the owl.

The dog looked up but he still didn't see them. "Where are you? I can't see you."

"We're here to tell you something," Hank said, slowly, with a certain pride. "Jasper, you go ahead."

The dog raced around the tree, stiff-legged, bouncing and barking. "I'm listening, go ahead."

Jasper tried to think. Unlike the owl, he couldn't fly his way out of this mess. He had grave and serious doubts that he could talk sense to the barbarian dog but it would seem that was his only chance at the moment.

"There's going to be a fire in the big man's bedroom," he said.

"A fire! When? Where?" The dog had finally spotted them. "Hey! Aren't you that cat I almost got today?"

"In the big man's bedroom. He just told you," Hank said.

"Okay, okay. But when?" The dog yelped and wiggled with excitement. Jasper got a sinking sensation in his gut when he saw the big man trotting up beside the dog.

"We don't know when," Hank continued patiently. "Sometime soon. You've got to keep watch for it."

The big man reached the dog and thumped the heavy triangle of his head with real appreciation.

"Good work, boy. Knew you'd find him." The big man didn't sound like his daytime voice. He spoke like his mouth was numb as he scanned the tree.

The dog laughed and danced. "I found them. I found them. There they are. Two of them. Don't you see them?"

The big man dropped all the rocks but one and turned so one shoulder faced the tree. He cocked his arm back and swayed.

"Son of a bitch wake me out of a sound sleep," the man muttered.

Jasper flattened his body and crawled to the opposite side of the tree trunk.

"Take off," he said to Hank.

"Why?" Hank was confused.

"That's a rock," Jasper said, focusing on moving smooth and long, "and it will hurt you."

"Oh?" Hank still didn't get it.

"Just do it — I'm going higher." He hoped and prayed the foliage would hide him and that his claws would hold and his balance would stay true. The thought of tumbling to the ground gave him a chill. He climbed quickly, carefully. He stopped to glance back and noticed two things: Hank hadn't moved an inch and the big man was staring directly at the big owl.

"Hey dog," Hank was saying. "Talk some sense in the man. Can't you make him understand we're here to help?"

"I'm trying." The dog shouted and laughed with dark pleasure. "Just keep talking. I think he's beginning to come around."

There was a sudden flipping through the leaves. The big man must have thrown the rock because there was a dull thud and Hank screamed in pain and shock. Jasper cringed and tried to flatten into a shadow. A small stinging voice in his head said that if he were any kind of hero, he would try to jump on the big man's head and scratch his eyes out. He thought he heard a faint muffled whirring and prayed it was Hank moving to safety.

"Hank," he whispered.

"Got him!" the man said to the dog. He squatted to pick up another rock and nearly lost his balance.

The dog sniffed and raced around the base of the tree. "You got him, boss! You got a piece of him. I heard it." The dog quivered with excitement and joy.

Jasper felt queasy, like when he had eaten too much grass. He clung to the tree and tried to take deep breaths.

"But there's two of them." The dog jumped up and braced his front paws on the tree trunk. "I don't think you got both."

The man peered into the tree for a few long minutes. Jasper could hear the sound of his own breath and thought surely the rasping sound and the stink of his fear would give him away.

"That'll take care of him," the man said. "Damned spooky owl." He dropped the rock and patted the dog. "Good work, boy. Let's go back to bed."

He turned and started walking a crooked, unsteady path toward the house.

"But we're not finished!" The dog jumped and barked. "That mangy cat's still up there. Gotta get him!"

"Come on, Max," the man said.

The dog quivered and yipped with frustration. "But he's still up there."

"Max," the big man said and his voice had a menacing gravity. The dog snapped to attention and bounded off after the man. By the time they reached the house and closed the door behind them, Jasper could feel all his hope and energy and optimism draining from him like he'd been asleep, spellbound in some baffling dream and was now waking back up to his ragged, cold life.

What a fiasco. Trying to help two wretched beings that didn't even know they needed help — and look what it got them. *Where is Hank? The big dummy. If he'd only just done what I told him to do. Of course he didn't and now he's wounded and bleeding somewhere, maybe dying. He shouldn't have come. I shouldn't have come, shouldn't have let him get involved.*

Chapter 5

ASPER SEARCHED THE NIGHT SKY, ready to confront the one who started all this. He wanted her to see her handiwork. Too many trees and too many lights obscured his view but that didn't stop him from talking to her. She had to be up there, watching all of this from her safe, comfortable distance.

"Is this what you wanted?" he said. "What you had in mind? I did the best I knew how. Whose idea was it to send Hank? Why didn't you get him ready? You saw what happened. He walked right into them. Why did you let that happen?"

The rage and pain balled up inside Jasper's gut like a giant knotted hairball. The knot tightened and clenched until he could hardly breathe and he thought the pain would stop his heart until a whimpering cry escaped him. He shook his head.

Everything was all out of whack. Cats weren't supposed to cry. Especially over owls. Cats and owls weren't supposed to be friends. Everybody knew that.

"So we're friends?" It was Hank's voice drifting down to him, a little shaky but clear.

Jasper stood up and braced his paws on the trunk to look over his head. A blocky shadow a few branches above him gave a single hushed *hoo* and Jasper climbed up to sit beside the owl.

The big bird looked a little shrunken, his face pinched, but the big yellow eyes were steady as ever. A small dark splotch stained the tweedy gray-brown of the feathers on his chest.

"Are you all right?" Jasper leaned in for a good deep sniff of him. He smelled okay. Scared and a little bloodied by the sharp rock but no scent of death on Hank.

"I've been better." Hank spoke in choppy, short-winded bursts. "It hurts." He cocked his head and peered closely at Jasper. "Why did he do that? You knew what he was going to do. How did you know? How did you know and I didn't?" The effort of all the talking clearly exhausted the owl and he crumpled a little.

"Just take it easy. Don't get yourself all worked up." Jasper watched the bird closely. "I've seen people throw rocks before. I knew he was going to do it because I know that man." He closed his eyes. "He's a bad one."

"So that's why you're helping him." Hank nodded sagely.

"No!" Jasper was shocked by the thought, by the strength of his own reaction. "I'm not helping him because he's bad. If I had any choice about it, I wouldn't help him at all."

"But he needs help," the injured owl said.

"I guess so, but I don't know how to help someone like that. Does it help him to scare him enough so he comes out of his house with his evil dog and blasts his rocks at you and me?"

"Maybe the dog believed us," Hank said.

"And maybe pigs can fly," Jasper said.

"Pigs flying?" Hank said. "You've seen it?"

"Aw Hank, grow up. That dog hates us. Especially me. He's tried to kill me twice, three times if you count tonight. He's a vicious, hard-hearted bully whose only pleasure is in hurting things."

"How do you know that?"

"How can you not know that?" Jasper was getting frustrated. "Didn't you see how he acted? He lied to you. He wanted to keep you distracted long enough for the man to get a clear shot at you. Don't be naïve."

Hank was silent for a moment. "There were other thoughts."

"You could read his thoughts?" Jasper said.

"Not like yours. Yours are clear and specific and I get the feelings that go with the thoughts. With him, I just got these waves of feeling. The thoughts were faint but the feelings were strong. Waves of feeling." Hank spoke slowly, thoughtfully.

"And what exactly was the vicious oaf feeling while he stood under the tree and waited for his big fat beastmaster to knock us in the head?"

"He was excited. Thrilled to be pleasing the man. But he was also afraid," Hank said.

"Afraid! What did he have to be afraid of?" Jasper said.

"Us," Hank said. "Me and you. He thinks we know things that he doesn't. He thinks we're magic. He envies us. He knows that we know the moon and that she's the closest thing we'll ever have to a master while he and his kind are bound to humans."

Jasper studied the straight lines of the house, the play of light dancing once again at the man's bedroom window. Could it be true? Could that be the reason the dog hated him so violently?

"It's true," said Hank.

"Well, what about the man? What was he thinking?" Jasper said.

Hank sighed and stretched out his wings. He winced and brought them back to his sides. He took a long pensive moment before he answered.

"The big man is afraid."

Jasper laughed, a quiet elegant cat laugh. "No."

"For the man, his anger is his claws, his talons and wings. But the big angry man is afraid, just like the dog."

Jasper shook his head. "Afraid of you and me, I suppose, just like the dog."

Hank blinked and settled his feathers. "The big man's afraid of time. Minutes, hours, seconds. He feels the weight of time on him so heavy he can barely breathe. The thing about him is, he doesn't even know it. I could feel it so strong, it almost knocked me off the window ledge." He stopped for a minute and preened his wing carefully. "I don't have much experience with people. I could be wrong."

Jasper said nothing, just watched the owl look back at the house and blink like a child. Like the boy used to blink, slowly, with an aching vulnerability.

"He's lying in that bed, watching that box and the terror's just rolling off him, piling up in that room like autumn leaves. But he's not seeing. He's watching the box and drinking something numbing and all the fear in his body never moves into his thoughts; he doesn't let it. He makes up all these rules about everything and gets mean as a badger when one of them gets broken. So he never lets himself think he's afraid. He knows it, of course, but he never thinks it out loud." Hank stopped again and looked up into the night sky, searching.

"I never knew that was possible. That's why I stayed on the ledge so long. I couldn't believe what he was doing. Do all people do that?"

Jasper sat pondering for a long grateful moment that he didn't know firsthand what it would be like to step into the big man's interior life, to know his thoughts and feelings like a second skin. He shuddered.

"I have no idea," he answered Hank's question. Then he thought of the boy and his brown-eyed love. The kisses and whispers and hugs and tears the boy had given him without screening or filters or distraction. Undiluted and whole. He thought of the frosty-haired woman — the hum of satisfaction and affection and pleasure she had given him so freely. The way she'd stood up for him with the dog and later both dog and man.

"No. They're not all like that. Not at all."

Both cat and owl were silent for a long moment.

"How are you feeling?" Jasper asked.

"A little better," Hank said.

"What do you think we should do now?" Jasper looked at the house, the flickering window. Something in what Hank had said had shifted the resistant hardness in his heart and mind. It didn't seem to matter anymore what the big man and the dog did. He and Hank had a job to do, regardless.

"I'm not sure," Hank replied and there was a big yawn in his voice.

"Maybe we should just stay here a little while. I don't know if tonight's the night, but you go ahead and take a little rest. I'll keep an eye out."

Hank nodded, eyes closing.

"Now, you won't fall off the branch or anything?" Jasper was a little nervous. He didn't know how much help he'd be if the big bird fell to the ground.

Hank shook his head no.

"Back in a minute," Jasper whispered to the drowsing owl.

He picked his way carefully down the tree. Climbing up wasn't hard — it was the getting down that was the hard part. That's when he was most likely to lose a claw. Finally he reached the ground and he stretched luxuriously. He felt the familiar rumble of hunger in his belly and he thought how easy it was to become accustomed to regular meals.

He stood in the grass, damp now with dew, and absorbed the smells, the night sounds. Something moved in the grass and Jasper pounced. He came up empty, as usual, saw the grass move and hopped again. Nothing. He scanned the grass, ever the hopeful hunter.

"I'm proud of you." The moon's voice was rich and rounded as cream.

He breathed her words in and let them roll down the stretch of his spine to the tip of his tail, the tapered edge of every claw. She was proud of him. He rolled to his back and squirmed in the grass like a cat worm.

"I need for you to keep taking care of Hank," she said.

He stopped wiggling and sat up on his haunches. "The bird has led a sheltered life," he said.

"He needs you."

"Why me?" Jasper said. "I'm not complaining, just curious."

"Why not?" she said.

"He doesn't need me. He was doing fine on his own before he met me. Probably a lot better in fact. He's never seen anybody throw a rock before tonight and now he's been hit by one. I know he needs me until we get through tonight, but beyond that? You don't mean anything beyond that, do you?"

The moon said nothing.

Jasper sat, his tail whipping unconsciously until the dull ache at the end reminded him to stop and he curled it round him to lick and nurse and groom. He started with his tail and continued up his back legs while the questions bounced around inside his head. *What did she mean? Surely not that we're supposed to stay together indefinitely. How would the two of us ever find a home? Who will ever take both of us in? Will I ever see the boy again?* He was working on his front paws and face when the sharp smell of fire reached him.

Jasper bounced up and ran back to the tree.

"Hank!" he called. He could just make out the stocky shape of the owl high in the branches.

"Hank!" He called again, louder, his heart pounding hard in his temples.

"Hmm?" Hank finally mumbled.

"Fire, Hank. Can't you smell it?"

"Oh," the owl said and Jasper could tell that he still wasn't quite awake. Panic rippled through him. He was going to have to handle it himself, but how?

He trotted quickly to the big man's house, and moved to the bedroom window. The light still flickered inside and Jasper sat for a few long seconds, watching the light, wanting the dog to wake up.

The seconds stretched to minutes and the fire smell got stronger although he didn't see any smoke yet. The window was too high for him to reach. Fear shivered through him and he circled the house, looking for an opening, an idea. The house was shut up tight as a clenched fist and nothing came to him.

He stood outside the window, his heart thumping, sick with frustration. He looked up and caught sight of the slivery moon, half-hidden behind a puffy clump of clouds.

"What am I supposed to do now?" he howled. "Tell me! I don't know what to do. I can't fly. I can't get inside. HELP!"

Inside the room, he heard a thumping clatter, then the sleepy frightened voice of the dog. "What's going on? Who's that?"

"Wake up! Wake up! WAKE UP!" Jasper screamed.

"Help!" called the dog with terror in his voice. "It's a fire. I can't wake him up. Help! Help!"

Jasper stood in the yard, stiff with fear and a terrible uncertainty. What to do? He thought of the frosty-haired woman. He might be able to wake her but to get her back here in time would be a long shot. He tried to think slowly, with clarity.

"Just calm down for a minute," he told the dog. The smell of fire was very strong now and he could see wisps of black smoke through the window.

"Calm down?" the dog yelped. "How can I calm down? This place is on fire!"

"Just talk to me," Jasper said. "Have you tried to lick him?"

"Lick him?" The dog moaned. "No, of course not."

"Try it!" Jasper commanded.

There was quiet for a few minutes. He thought he heard the man mumble and groan but then there was nothing but the quiet of the night.

"He's passed out. Won't wake up! Help me!" The dog's voice was shrill with panic.

"Bark!" Jasper said.

"I am barking!" the dog said. "He just mumbles and rolls over."

"Bite him," Jasper said.

"Bite him?" the dog yelped. "But he'll beat me."

Jasper yowled in frustration. "Would you rather be beaten or burned up?"

"The fire's getting bigger. It's hard to breathe. I'm scared." The dog gasped and coughed and Jasper shivered.

"Bite him!" Jasper said. "Hard! You've got to bite him hard enough to wake him up. Do it!"

The dog moaned and cried and the seconds ticked away. There was a long silence in which Jasper thought he heard muted crackling and snapping of what had to be the growing fire and he stared fiercely at the window, willing the dog to do what he had said.

Then the man swore, the dog yelped in pain and there was a loud thump and clatter. The man kept talking, his voice hoarse and garbled at first then thin with fear.

"Fire! FIRE!" he yelled.

Jasper could hear doors opening and the heavy thumping of feet. When the man and dog finally stumbled into the back yard, coughing and choking, he sighed with relief.

The man pounded the dog's side, hugged him close.

"You saved my life, buddy. Bit a damn hole in my arm, but you saved my life."

The dog panted and wheezed and caught Jasper's eye from the embrace of the big man's arms.

The man released the dog and stood. "Gotta call the fire department." He stumbled off toward the neighbors' dark houses.

The dog sat, still breathing in big heaving gulps. Jasper could feel his eyes as he moved across the yard. The cold familiar shadow of dog fear fell across Jasper's heart and he began to slink toward the cover of the tree where Hank still roosted. He'd saved the dog's life and the dog knew it, but he didn't like the feel of the dog's eyes on him and who knew what went on in a canine mind?

He'd almost reached the tree when he heard and felt the pounding. The dog moved between him and the tree.

"I want to know why," the dog said, his heavy head low, sniffing at Jasper.

"Why what?" Jasper said.

"Why did you do it?" the dog said.

Jasper shrugged. "Why not?"

The dog laughed, a short staccato bark. "Lots of reasons. I tried to kill you." He peered close at Jasper with bloodshot eyes. "I still want to, you know."

For a reason Jasper couldn't name, he didn't quite believe the dog. "Do you?"

The dog snorted and sat down. "I just don't get it."

Jasper sighed. "I really don't get it either."

"I still don't like you." The dog curled his lip.

"Likewise." Jasper flexed his claws.

"But you saved my life." The dog cocked his head. "His, too. So I won't try to kill you anymore. It just wouldn't seem right."

"That would be nice."

"But don't expect any help from me." The dog stood up and shook himself. "You get into situations with other dogs, you're on your own."

Jasper nodded.

"One thing I want to know." The dog squinted closely at him.

Jasper waited.

"How did you know it was going to happen? The fire," the dog said. "I mean, the owl acted like you knew it. Did he tell you? Was he the one who first knew it?"

Jasper glanced up at the sky. The moon was in clear sight again, closer to the horizon, a gleaming smile in the dark face of the sky.

"You'd be surprised at what he knows," he said.

The dog nodded, still not completely convinced. He turned away and started to trot toward the house. He stopped.

"You got a name?" the dog said.

"Jasper."

"I'm Max," he said. "Stay out of my yard, okay? I'd have to chase you and all. For the big guy. He hates cats. Ever since the wife left him. Took her two cats and their daughter and moved to someplace called Michigan."

"Really?" Jasper said.

"That's why he's got me. He saved my life, you know. I was two hours away from the needle when he picked me out and brought me home." The dog resumed trotting. "Watch out for the Dobie two streets over," he tossed over his shoulder.

The two of them traveled slowly back to the woods, Jasper limping slightly and Hank flying short distances with frequent rests. They stopped at the small gurgling creek for Jasper to take a long lapping drink and enjoy the coolness of air just next to the water.

When they reached the fort, Jasper climbed into his tight inside pocket and Hank moved to the upper reaches of a nearby oak. Jasper curled his tail around his nose and as he closed his eyes and felt that light delicious drift into the blurry edges of sleep, he heard Hank's hoot. It sounded deeply fatigued but rich with pride and something else that Jasper was just too relaxed to consider, and so he took a big cleansing breath and slept, oddly comforted in the cool, relentless dawn.

Chapter 6

ASPER SLEPT FOR THE BETTER PART OF a day and a half, a deep, indulgent sleep that embarrassed him; it was uncatlike to sleep so deeply and so long.

The voices woke him. Two boys and a girl, young voices and light footsteps humming through the hard-packed floor of the fort. He peered through the gaps in the fort ceiling.

"It's great, isn't it?" one of the boys said. His voice was insistent, quick-paced.

"Who built it?" said the girl. She knocked on one of the inside boards and Jasper could feel the reverberation in his bones.

"Who knows?" said the confident boy. "Who cares?"

"They might care," said the girl. "They might not like us using their fort."

"Well, they're not here now. And they haven't been here in a while," said the boy. "I've been checking."

There was a period of quiet and the other boy said something so softly that even Jasper couldn't make out the words.

"What?" said the insistent boy. "What did you say, Nathan? Say it out loud so I can hear you."

Nathan whispered again to the girl.

"Come on, baby. Speak up. Why can't you just say it so we can all hear you?"

"Maybe he doesn't want you to hear him," said the girl.

Confident boy paused then spoke slowly, deliberately. "Maybe we should dig a hole and dump him in it."

He continued, "Maybe he's too much of a baby to be here." Jasper watched the confident boy approach Nathan. He took a big pinch of the quiet boy's cheek between his thumb and forefinger and twisted.

"Tyler!" The girl punched the big boy in the shoulder. He held on and Jasper could hear the grunts and feel the light thumping of Nathan trying to loosen the grip and step away.

"What are you gonna do, baby boy?" Tyler twisted the small boy's flesh until glints of tears and fury shone in his eyes.

Jasper leaped to the ground and crept behind Tyler like an oily shadow. He twisted through the boy's legs then stiffened, making his body a tight hard *S* around Tyler's ankles.

"Wha...?" Tyler jerked his head around to look behind him as he released his grip on Nathan's cheek. He flailed his arms, trying to regain his balance.

Nathan stumbled forward, smacking his head into the center of Tyler's chest. The big boy went down hard.

"Owwwww," Tyler moaned. Nathan stood poised beside the girl, both ready to run. "Owwwwwww," the boy on the ground continued to moan. "What was that? Who tripped me?"

Nathan and the girl looked at Jasper who sat a few yards away, grooming himself, nonchalant and disinterested. The children looked at each other and smiled. Jasper walked around to the tree trunk side of the fort and climbed back up to his perch. Through the cracks, he watched the big boy flop to his stomach and continue to moan. The other children circled him from a cautious few feet.

"Are you okay?" said the girl.

"Does it look like I'm okay? I think that rabbit broke my butt."

Rabbit? thought Jasper, insulted.

Tyler pushed himself up to his hands and knees. "Where'd it go?"

The girl shrugged and said, "Maybe a groundhog."

Oh that's better, reflected Jasper.

Nathan looked doubtful. Tyler stood up and pressed both hands to his bottom. "Groundhog, huh?" he said.

"Or a snake," the girl offered hopefully.

Tyler shuddered. "Are you serious? Did you see a snake?"

Nathan looked at the girl then nodded aggressively. "Snake. Big snake."

"Thick as your arm," she said.

Tyler glanced around him. "No big deal," he said. "I've gotta go."

"It's only 3:30, Tyler. I thought you didn't have to be home until 4:00," said the girl.

"My mom's coming home early today. I've got to do my homework so we can go out to eat." He started to shuffle away, then thought better of it and began to lift his feet up with care.

He moved out of sight and the sound of him rustling through the woods faded into the muffled shush of the summer breeze. Nathan and his sister Brittany looked at each other and began to giggle.

"SNAKE, Bree!" The boy pointed and jumped.

She shrieked back at him, "It's right BEHIND you! Don't fall on your BUTT!"

They collapsed in laughter, pushing and nudging each other like puppies. Jasper smiled a secret cat smile and began to purr softly to himself. Maybe things were beginning to go his way. Maybe one of these two would be enough like his boy for the occasional treat of canned food every now and again. Maybe more often than now and again. Maybe a clean, warm place to sleep.

There was a soft whirring and a great rush of air. Jasper flattened, hoping it was Hank.

"Did you see the little people down there?" Hank nodded his head toward the boy and girl.

"Indeed I did," said Jasper. He stood and stretched. "Think I'll go down and say hello."

"Are you sure?" said Hank, twisting his neck to watch the children. "What if they have rocks?"

"They don't," said Jasper. "I've been watching them." He winked at the owl. "They might just be looking for a cat to take home."

Hank blinked rapidly. "And you would do that?"

Jasper sighed. "It is my fondest dream to be pampered and fattened and spoiled beyond belief. Lots of cats get treated that way, you know."

"No!"

"Yes!"

"Whatever for?" said Hank.

"Whatever for what?" said Jasper, walking to the roof edge and watching the children. He needed to get down there before they walked away.

"Well, both! Why do they do that and why would you want it?"

Jasper looked at the ground and crouched to jump. "Look, Hank, I'll explain it to you later. I've got to go right now." He leaped.

"I'll keep a close eye on you from up here," Hank called out. "Just say if you need help."

Jasper walked toward the children and they watched him. The boy stood still, head cocked. Jasper noticed that the boy was different than any child he'd seen; his face looked different, features slightly distorted, and he moved with jerky, abrupt motions. When he spoke, his words were all run together.

"Hey look," Brittany said. "There's that cat."

"Snake cat!" Nathan said.

She stretched out a hand to Jasper. "Here kitty." Jasper

approached and sniffed her hand delicately, politely. She smelled of powdery tart candy and cloves. She stroked his head.

The boy squatted and squinted at Jasper.

"You should thank him, Nathan," Brittany said. "He's a sweet cat. I like him."

The boy's hand went to his cheek, still streaked with red. He reached toward Jasper. "Here kitty."

Jasper was enjoying Brittany's caresses and he gave Nathan a slit-eyed look, not sure about the boy and the odd jerky way he moved.

Nathan wiggled his fingers. "Good kitty."

Jasper stretched his neck to sniff his hand. Nathan smelled like wood smoke and cookies. His touch was softer and more tentative than Brittany's.

"Who do you think he belongs to?" she said.

Nathan shook his head.

"He's pretty skinny," said Brittany, and Jasper gave her a long, slow eye kiss for noticing. He rubbed his head against her leg with hope and gave a pitiful meow.

"We've already got two cats," she said mournfully. "Chloe and Joey."

Jasper stood between them and hummed deep in his chest, enjoying the feel of their small hands. There were things worse than starving. Living wild and untouched, for instance.

"Do you have anything to eat, Nathan?" Brittany said.

He looked doubtful and searched his pockets. He offered the findings on his palm to Jasper: old cookie crumbs and a scarred Lifesaver. Jasper sniffed politely and declined, rubbing his head against the boy's thumb. The boy glowed.

"Isn't he sweet? Chloe and Joey don't let you touch them like that." Brittany smiled.

Nathan patted Jasper's head with an open hand, a little hard, but Jasper didn't mind.

"Where does he get water?" Brittany looked around, her eyes

wide and distraught. She hugged Jasper with two stalky arms and pressed her cheek against his coat.

Jasper was trying to look pitiful but brave when the mind picture hit. He saw the girl at night, outside in a silent stretch of land studded with blocks of stone. Some of the stone blocks stood up in neat rows; some were mostly buried so that only the smooth face showed, but all were deeply etched with characters. The place was quiet, but it was very dark and the girl was terrified, shrieking wildly, running into the stones and knocking over flowers, figurines, and other small items that had been left on the stones.

Jasper shuddered, closed his eyes and tried to concentrate when the image dissolved as quickly as it had come. He studied the girl's face. She was perhaps a little older than his boy had been, with a round face and bold, light eyes. Her hair was light too, almost colorless. *What was she so afraid of? What was the place and why was she there?*

"It's a place where humans bury their dead," Hank said, from the top of the fort.

At the sound of his voice, the boy stiffened and searched the trees. "Hear that?" said Nathan. "Owl?"

Brittany cocked her head, listening.

"Where they bury their dead?" Jasper was perplexed. "Why would they want to do that?" The only thing he ever buried was his daily business.

"Don't know. But I've seen a few of them," Hank said.

Nathan took a few steps away so he could see the top of the fort. He pointed. "Look, Bree," he said, shrill with excitement. "Big one."

"The boy can hear you, Hank." Jasper wasn't sure if this was a good thing.

"I know. I'm going to go find something to eat," Hank said, then he stretched out his wings and with that soft whirring, launched himself from the tree and disappeared into the woods.

Nathan shaded his eyes against the late afternoon sun and watched Hank fly away. Jasper butted his head against Nathan's leg and the boy dropped to one knee, stroking Jasper with his heavy flat hands.

Brittany stared at Jasper.

"Why aren't you afraid?" Brittany said to the cat. He purred and pushed his head against the boy's hands. "Cats are supposed to be afraid of owls. Aren't they, Nathan? A big owl like that one could fly off with a kitten."

She reached out and gently squeezed Jasper's sides. "And probably you too, skinny as you are."

Nathan scratched Jasper right at the base of his tail. "Friends. Owl and the cat."

Brittany squinted at Jasper. "Maybe so."

Jasper blinked at the girl and boy. They were sharp ones. He still wasn't sure if it was a good thing or a dangerous thing that they were so attuned and yet oblivious. The image of her in the dark place with the stones still bothered him. She had been so frightened.

The children stayed until the shadows of the trees stretched long and the fresh chill scent of the woods at night began to drift around them. They walked and Jasper followed at a hopeful distance, not directly under their feet like a foolish dog, as much as he may have wanted to. A cat had to have a little self-respect.

They left the woods and walked by the big angry man's house. Jasper scanned the yard, thinking of the dog and the last brutal chase, despite the dog's words the night of the fire. How far could one trust a dog?

The children walked on, down one block, then a turn, then a stretch of several blocks with more of the same kind of houses: big and square and neatly contained like bricks in a wall. Just looking at them gave Jasper hope. Surely there was someone tucked inside one of those boxy nests in need of fine feline companionship. The homes looked so big and prosperous; he could just imagine the food inside. They probably had rooms full of it. Piles of tuna and salmon, chicken legs, and big glistening chunks of meat. He moaned to himself with the lovely gluttonous thought of it.

Brittany stopped by a fenced-in yard. She pushed a hand through the posts of a split-rail fence toward a thick-bodied dog with a golden coat that approached the girl with an open-mouthed smile and a baseball bat of a tail swinging in slow circles.

Brittany turned to watch Nathan.

"You don't have to be afraid of all dogs, Nathan." She shaded her eyes against the late afternoon sun. "Come here and pet him."

Nathan held his hands behind his back and shook his head from side to side.

Brittany caught sight of Jasper hanging behind.

"Hey," she said and squatted down. "Did you follow us?"

Jasper stretched and took a few languid steps toward her.

"You're hungry, aren't you, skinny boy?" She rubbed his head. "Well, come on then." She began striding down the street on her spidery legs, stopping to kick the occasional rock and wait for Nathan to catch up. Jasper trotted behind.

"Brittany! Nathan!" Someone was calling the children from close by.

Another block and a half and they were climbing the driveway of a light brick house on a hill. There was a tall woman on the back steps.

"There you are!" She reached for the boy and hugged him. "What's that on your cheek?"

Nathan mumbled and wriggled out of her grasp.

"Brittany? What happened to his face?" The tall woman followed Brittany into the house.

"Nothing, Mom, we were just fooling around." Brittany's voice grew fainter as she disappeared into the house.

Jasper sat down in the grass and smelled deeply of the fresh evening smells floating through the air. Someone was barbequing down the block and the whiffs of the roasting meat were intoxicating. He looked up at the sky, still lit with the streaky trails of the sun making her extravagant daily exit. He scanned for the moon but saw no curving hint of her presence.

"What do you think you're doing, Mangy?" Jasper turned his head slowly to see the source of the voice. It belonged to a plump gray feline with grass-green snake eyes crouched a few feet from him, her tail whipping from side to side.

"Don't be so rude, Chloe. You're always so harsh with visitors." The second voice came from his other flank. A lustrous ebony cat stood there, ears forward with interest.

The gray cat, with flattening ears and an expanding tail, started growling a low-pitched hard whine. The black cat took two soft steps toward Jasper and then the gray one jumped on him, all flashing claws and teeth.

Jasper screamed and slashed back and he and the gray cat tumbled in the yard, a small cyclone of spitting, yowling rage. Dimly, he could hear the back door slam and the girl's cries to stop. Inside the tangle, he bit and scratched and angled for position. It was only a few seconds but it felt far too long when he finally cleared himself and hit solid ground with both haunches. He coiled and took a towering first jump, running hard past swing sets and through flowerbeds, hoping the soft close thumping he heard was the sound of his own heart and not the gray grump on his heels. His lungs burned and his bad leg and tail ached; he was built for sprints, not distance. He stopped running and pivoted, his back curled into a hard horseshoe, fur puffed to twice his size to face his pursuer.

No one was there. Jasper sank into the grass, panting and weak with relief. There was a stinging place on his head; he licked his paw and tried to rub it clean.

"Are you all right?" The familiar voice from the nearby sugar maple jolted his tired heart into another frenzy of hard beating.

"Of course I'm all right, Hank. Why do you always have to sneak up on me like that?" Jasper said irritably.

"I didn't sneak up," Hank said. "I've been behind you the whole time." He peered down at Jasper. "Why was that cat so hateful? Did she hurt you?"

"Not much." Jasper drew himself together and looked around.

They were deep in someone's back yard he didn't recognize.

"Looks like you're bleeding on your head there, right in front of your ear."

"I know," said Jasper. "It's fine."

"Why did she attack you like that, Jasper? Did you do something to her?"

"Oh, Hank." Jasper sighed. He was bone-sore and hungry and didn't feel like explaining the jealous and possessive nature of cats to an unworldly owl at the moment.

"What's unworldly?" Hank said.

"Unworldly's when you don't know much about the way things are and you ask a lot of annoying questions instead of trying to figure things out by yourself," Jasper snapped.

There was a long silence. Jasper tried hard to fan his frustration into justification for his harsh words, but he couldn't.

"Hank, I'm sorry," he said. "I'm just not feeling too well. I could really do with something to eat."

"What would you like?" Hank said.

"Don't tease me," Jasper moaned.

"Do you like shrews? Little plump field mice?"

Jasper felt his stomach twist and churn. "The truth of it is that I'm not much of a game-eater."

"No?" Hank stopped. Both of them could feel his question hovering between them like a hummingbird. Hank hesitated. "So you like human food," he said carefully.

"Yes," Jasper said.

"Human food like they eat?" Hank said.

"Well, that can be very good, the meat especially, but what's also good is the food they make just for cats." Jasper's mouth watered at the thought of it.

"They make food just for cats?" Hank said.

"It's the moon's own truth," Jasper said and as he did, glanced overhead. The familiar gleaming curve of her face smiled down.

"Do they make food for owls?" Hank said.

Jasper cocked his head. "I've never heard of it but it's entirely possible."

The two of them sat in silence for a long moment, watching the sky together. The moon seemed particularly happy tonight; Jasper could feel the waves of satisfaction wash over him like a gentle rain.

"She is well tonight," Hank murmured.

"True," said Jasper. "Glad somebody's feeling good." The thought soured. "Of course what would you have to worry about when you're the moon?"

"I can think of a few things," the moon said quietly.

Jasper froze. She had never spoken to him in the presence of another, only when it was just the two of them alone. It felt uncomfortable. He glanced at Hank to see if he had heard. The big owl was gazing dreamily at the horizon, eyes half-shut.

"It's all right," she said. "It will be all right."

The scent of chicken roasting on a back yard grill drifted by them and Jasper closed his eyes and licked his lips.

"I've got an idea," Hank said.

"Don't do anything foolish, Hank. I can always go to the dumpster behind the chicken place. It's just a couple of miles away." He cringed inside at the thought. The food was tolerable, sometimes pieces of biscuit and cold fried chicken, but it was the shame of it he hated. Digging in a dumpster was nothing for a respectable cat to do.

Hank had already lifted his wings and disappeared into the dusk. Jasper could hear the girl still calling him in the distance; she sounded upset. *Maybe tomorrow I'll swing by to see her.* Now wasn't the time. Funny how female cats were always the ones that gave him a hard time. As a kitten, he'd hoped to grow up like his father, a smoldering black tom who stalked the world like a small stern tiger. Jasper shook his head. You had to have the right attitude; it was all in the attitude, his father had told Jasper, but somehow it never worked for Jasper quite the same way.

He got his bearings and started to make his way toward the chicken place. His head was sore and his leg ached but his mood was upbeat. He was crossing the back yard of a split level with cream-colored siding when he recognized the yard of the frosty-haired woman. Maybe she was out and about.

She was watering a leggy stand of sunflowers in her back yard, cigarette in hand, sweeping the hose over the black-eyed golden faces in slow arcs. He hesitated, because of the water, and then made his way to sit behind her in the yard where she'd be sure to see him when she turned back to the house.

He sat and watched the soft, tentative throbbing of the fireflies and thought how much he loved the early evening. The air was fresh and alive with all the scents that had been dulled by heat or light. Evening was when things started to get interesting. The moon was at her most accessible, sometimes huge and yellow on the horizon like she was leaning down to take a good close look at Jasper's world.

It was then she seemed the most vulnerable to Jasper, with her naked, smudged face and her inevitable drifting, higher and smaller as the night stretched on. She must know how it felt not to be the pretty one; was the sun always changing her brilliant shape? No, the sun was always on display, always preening and posturing like certain pedigreed cats he knew, confident that approving eyes were always watching. The moon was moody, always changing in shape and expression but at least she noticed things.

He sighed and looked toward the window where Precious watched him, her features pinched with dislike.

"Hello handsome," the woman said. "Haven't seen you since that dog got after you. What's that on your head? You been fighting?"

He rubbed against her legs. She bent over to look at his head and that's when he saw Hank. He was soaring overhead with something gripped in one talon that looked like a short chunk of garden hose. He swooped in close and dropped his load a few feet away from Jasper and the woman. She jumped and squawked a little.

"Goodness gracious sakes alive," she said. "Is that a snake?" She took a few steps back.

Jasper trotted quickly to sniff at the thing in the grass. It smelled wonderful, and it looked like something he'd seen people eating in a bun: a hot dog, charred with the lines of the grill where it had been cooking.

Heavenly, Jasper thought as he took a bite. *Hot dogs from heaven.* "What's that?" The woman had moved beside him for a closer look. "A hot dog?" She looked at the stand of trees where Hank had flown.

"Hot dogs dropping out of the sky," the woman said. "Sakes alive." She knelt to stroke his back. "You're not hungry or anything, are you?"

Jasper's favorite things in the world were to eat and be petted. When they happened simultaneously, he felt like he might just melt into the ground.

The woman went inside the house, blocking Precious and her threats. He watched the beautiful bouffant cat lean against the legs of the woman, who kneeled to press a kiss on the smug lovely face. The generous woman came back with a bowl of fresh clear water and a pie pan piled high with dry cat food. Jasper meowed loudly, with tremendous appreciation before he started to crunch on the food. The woman squatted to rub his back again.

"You've got a hard time of it, don't you fella? Dogs chasing you, housecats and big lunkheads hating you, living on whatever drops out of the sky," she said as she rubbed him. "What you need is a good solid home. Somebody to take care of you."

He stopped eating and gave her a big, slow eye kiss. How perceptive she was.

Jasper purred and started to crunch again. How lovely it was to have people feeding him, worrying about his well-being. He'd like to follow up on the home idea with her but he was too concerned with eating to pursue it properly. He was crunching so loudly he almost missed the faint jingle of the choke collar and leash. The frosty-haired woman stiffened and twisted toward the sound. The big angry man and Max were standing at the back of the woman's driveway. The man held Max's leash with one hand, in the other he held what looked like a small triangular wooden box.

Jasper froze at the sight of them then sprang for the nearest tree, a mid-sized sugar maple. He scrambled up to a spot higher than he hoped the big angry man could reach.

"Hello," the big man said.

"Well, hello to you too." The woman put her hands on her hips, looked at Jasper and shook her head. "You're scaring my friend."

"Sorry about that, aren't we, Max?" The man looked down at the dog, then at the box in his other arm. "Don't mean to barge in on you but I just wanted to thank you for helping me out like you did the other night."

The frosty-haired woman took a few steps toward the man. "Well, you certainly don't need to do that. All I did was call the Fire Department."

The big man shrugged. "I know. But I wasn't in any shape to do it." He looked down at the ground. "I called that subcontractor you told me about, he's doing a great job on the house. Turns out the damage was pretty much confined to the bedroom. 'Course I'll have to live with the smell for a while."

"Could have been a lot worse," the woman said.

"Don't I know it." He held the box out to the woman. "Anyway, this is for you."

"Isn't it beautiful? I haven't had a birdhouse since my daughter lived at home. Before she got married and moved to the other side of the world." The woman took the box and turned it to look at it from all sides. "She loves birds."

"My daughter does too," the big man said. "'Course she's twelve so she's in love with horses now. Or she was, last time I saw her."

The frosty-haired woman looked at the big angry man for a long moment. The big man did look different somehow, Jasper had to admit. Previously, the very air around him would quiver with rage. Now he seemed quieter, more subdued. *Maybe fires were good for angry people.*

"Would you like something to drink, Mr. Peeler?" she said finally.

"That would be nice," the big man said. "Iced tea or soda. Not drinking the hard stuff anymore. Makes me do stupid things."

The woman looked at him and smiled. "I'll be right back." She started toward the back door and stopped. "Now you keep that dog leashed. I don't want him going after Freddie."

"Freddie?" the big man asked. "Who's Freddie?"

The woman pointed to Jasper. He cringed a little, hoping that Max and the man had forgotten about him.

"Oh," the man said. He eyed Jasper and the feel of his look was still hot, uncomfortable to the cat. "You thinking about taking that cat in?"

"Maybe," the woman said as she walked inside. "He needs a good home. Come on inside."

"You want to be careful where you put that birdhouse," the big man said. "Don't want it to be old fast Freddie's cafeteria. I'll give you a hand hanging it up if you like."

The man wrapped Max's leash around the railing on the frosty-haired woman's back steps and went inside. The woman left the heavy back door open, leaving only the storm door between Precious and the great outdoors while she and the big man sat at her kitchen table. Precious stood on her hind legs, cursing at Jasper and Max and pawing at the glass.

"It's okay." Max sprawled on the stoop, ignored Precious and spoke to Jasper. "I'm not going to chase you."

Despite the tickling finger of fear in his belly, Jasper made his way carefully down the tree. The pan of dry food still looked awfully tempting but he felt a little too tense to eat, with Max ten steps away and the big angry man just inside the door.

"Told you I'd leave you alone," said Max. "You act like you don't believe me."

"Nothing personal," Jasper said as he trotted away. "Old habits."

He headed back to the fort, stopping when he saw the bulky shadow of Hank in the branches of a massive water oak on the bank of the trickling creek between the neighborhood and the fort.

"Hank," he said. "You're my hero."

"Am I?" said Hank.

"Absolutely," said Jasper. "That hot dog really hit the spot."

"Is that what it was? Dog?"

"Well," said Jasper, with an uncomfortable feeling. "I don't think so."

"That's barbaric," said Hank. "Eating your friends? Aren't dogs great friends of theirs?" He cut his eyes at Jasper. "They don't eat cats, do they?"

Jasper swallowed hard. "Not that I know of." He paused. "I don't hear much about them eating owls either."

"Well, I should hope not," said Hank, his feathers a little puffed.

"Only the ones they catch stealing hot dogs." Jasper grinned at Hank until the joke registered with the big owl.

Hank nodded sagely. "Of course." He swiveled his head away. "And the cats that eat stolen hot dogs."

"Yes," said Jasper and he trotted home to the fort.

Chapter 7

THE MOON HAD RISEN HIGH IN THE SKY when Jasper woke with a wrenching sense of something horribly wrong. He listened hard and looked around carefully. Nothing seemed amiss, but there was that terrible empty feeling in his belly that had nothing to do with hunger.

"What's wrong?" said Hank from his perch in the nearby branches.

"I'm not sure," said Jasper. Then the image flashed in his mind, clear as if it were happening right in front of him. It was the girl Brittany, in the place with the stone blocks and flowers. She was with the boy Tyler and another boy that Jasper didn't recognize. The image faded and was replaced with an awful sense of helplessness.

"Where are they?" Jasper asked. "How do I find them?"

"I can take you," said Hank. "I know where they are."

For the second time that day, Jasper was deeply grateful to Hank. "Let's go!"

"What are we going to do when we get there?" said Hank.

"We'll figure it out," Jasper said, with more confidence than he felt. As he scrambled down the tree and struggled to keep sight of Hank, he tried to think of something, anything to take his mind off the idea that they were going to a place where dead people were buried. There were a lot of things he didn't understand about people but this idea of having all the dead in one place had to be one of the most baffling. The smell had to be monstrous.

Hank kept close, flying in short sweeps and calling out to make sure Jasper could follow but Jasper still struggled to keep up. They left the woods and on the other side of a wrought iron fence, Jasper could make out the shapes of the stone blocks he had seen in his mind picture, square and regular like big horse teeth. Jasper held his breath as long as he could, but when he finally took a deep taste of the air, he detected no smell of death.

As he slipped through the fence, he caught a glimpse of a pencil of light bobbing among the blocks. Ducking heads and stiff, furtive movements; it had to be the children.

"Do you think they'll have rocks?" Hank said, a slight quiver in his voice.

"No," said Jasper. "I don't think so."

"I'll go take a look," Hank said, and with a soft whoosh of wings, took off toward the light. Jasper watched him soar.

He's not afraid at all, he thought. *He's willing to fly into an uncertain situation just because I said so.* His mouth went dry at the thought of it. *Foolish, trusting owl. Need to talk to him about that.*

"What will you tell him?" The moon was distant but bright with purpose.

"He's so naïve," said Jasper. "It could be dangerous. Maybe you could tell him."

"He doesn't hear me," she said. "You know that."

"Why is that?" he asked. "Why is it that I can hear you and he can't?"

She was quiet. Jasper squinted at the small circle of light and pale faces. His night vision was excellent; the light was distracting. He could just make out Hank's stocky outline perched on one of the stone blocks. The faint warble of thin young voices drifted by him.

"I think you know," the moon said.

"But I don't," he said.

"But you do," she said.

"If I knew," Jasper said, "wouldn't I know it?"

The moon laughed and it was like a thousand joyous bells rang out in the uncertain night. There was nothing he hated more than being laughed at but he had never heard the moon laugh before. It was glorious.

Jasper looked over at the group in the midst of the stone blocks. Surely they had heard. But Hank didn't move and the children chattered on.

"How about a hint," he said.

The moon just smiled indulgently down on him.

Hank came swooping back to the fence, stiff with importance. "There are three of them. The girl and boy who were in the woods yesterday and another boy I don't recognize. The two boys are planning to play a trick on the girl – that's how they're thinking of it. The girl is very frightened and trying not to show it." He took a deep breath. "No rocks."

"What kind of trick?" Jasper said.

"They're going to hide and leave her alone in there."

Jasper shook his head. Both of them watched as the three young people stood and started walking deeper into the fenced area. One of the two boys gave a brief shout, the light clicked off and both boys broke into a run in opposite directions. Brittany stood and looked from one direction to another. She took a few tentative steps.

"Tyler? Ames?" she said.

Jasper and Hank looked at each other.

"I'll see if I can help her out," Jasper said. "How about if you go track those boys down and teach them a lesson?"

"What should I teach them?" Hank said.

"Give them a good scare. Fly right by their heads," Jasper said. "Hoot loudly and stare at them."

"Oh," said Hank. "Do you think that's okay?"

"I certainly do," Jasper said. "They've behaved badly and they need to be punished. Who else is going to do it?"

"Their parents?" Hank said.

"Do you see their parents anywhere around?" Jasper said. "Do whatever you like. I'm going to go see that girl." He bounded toward the girl, slowing to an easy walk when he got a few yards away.

"Tyler? Ames?" She was frozen in a half-crouch, wide-eyed and stiff limbed, saying the names over and over in a hoarse whisper. Her voice started to tremble.

"You guys, this isn't funny," she said. She took a few tentative steps, then began to run, all knees and elbows, in the direction that Tyler had taken. Jasper loped along behind, hoping she would run out of breath. Finally she stopped and he could hear her faint whimper bleed into the implacable night.

She took a deep breath that rolled into one sob, then another. Her small form clenched into a knot as she dropped to the ground and hugged her knees to her chest.

"Alicia?" She raised her head and whispered. Shoulders hunched, she peered around her in the darkness. "Alicia, are you here?"

Jasper tried a friendly meow but she was talking and didn't hear him. He waited for her to take a breath and tried again. This time, she heard him and screamed. She jumped to her feet. Jasper took a deep breath and gambled. He began meowing continuously to announce himself then took a few leaps forward to rub against her legs and sit in front of her in the moonlight. He blinked at her with affection.

She screamed again but it trailed off into a hum of recognition.

"Is it you?" she said and squatted cautiously. He meowed and butted his head into her hands, professing his keen delight in her company among dead buried people in the middle of the night.

"What are you doing here?" Brittany said as she rubbed his head. "Did Alicia send you?"

Funny you should ask, he thought and gazed up at her with pleasure. *Who's Alicia?* The tears were drying on her face and she didn't have that rigid look about her anymore. He allowed himself a sense of satisfaction and imagined that the moonlight had warmed with approval.

Then Hank hooted in the distance; a determined sound and the girl pulled Jasper close. She still smelled of candy, the dry powdery kind.

Hank hooted again, an insistent *hoo-hoo-hoooooooooooooooo*, that sounded like he was directly in front of them and not very pleased. Jasper could feel her stiffening. He gave her hand a small lick. Still squatting, she hugged him tighter and he squeaked.

Don't come too close now, he thought and hoped that Hank was listening. *I've just gotten her calmed down. You want to scare the boys, not her.*

"Ames!" The scream, shrill with fear, came from the right. "Ames, bring the light here!" The thumping of running feet sounded close by.

Jasper could feel the girl shrink down. They watched as Tyler stopped a short distance away, trembling and gasping, leaning against a massive marble block. Like a dark explosion, Hank flew out of the shadows and swept close by Tyler's face.

The boy whimpered and dropped to his knees, covering his head with his arms. Hank lighted on the marble block and fixed a menacing stare at him. Brittany shivered and buried her face in Jasper's neck.

"Please," said Tyler. "Leave me alone." His voice broke into dry, rasping sobs as he bent his head to the ground. "I'm sorry. I meant to give it back. I never meant to break it."

Hank looked at Jasper and Jasper blinked and gave a slight nod. Hank spread his wings and disappeared into the darkness. The boy lay still for a long few moments.

Brittany moved Jasper carefully from her lap, keeping her hands around his body, and stood, a little unsteady but still holding him close. She approached the collapsed boy.

"Tyler?" she said. "Are you all right?"

He didn't move at first. She came closer, holding Jasper like a talisman against the night. She stood over the boy and touched his leg with the toe of her shoe.

"Tyler?"

"That was my grandfather Bennington," he said without lifting his head.

"What?" Brittany said.

"I borrowed his knife and I broke it and I never told anybody." He sat up and stared in front of him. "Everybody thought he lost it because he was so old and always losing things. He knew."

"I don't think they like us coming here at night. Let's get out of here." She pulled at his arm with a free hand. Jasper could feel that he was a heavy load for her to carry but she wouldn't put him down.

Tyler stood and shook his head as if to clear it. "Who doesn't like us coming here? Where'd you get that cat?"

"He's special." She turned and started walked quickly. "Come on, let's go. I'll tell you about it later."

He stood for another minute, until they heard another *hoo-hoo-hoooooooooooooo* from not too far away.

"Where's Ames?" the boy said as he began to trot away.

"I don't know," she said, moving as quickly as she could. "He took off running the same time you did. Coincidence, I guess."

"Brittany," he said, slowing down to let her catch up. "I'm sorry. We thought it would be funny—"

"Funny ha-ha," she said, gripping Jasper tightly. He was definitely ready to get down but she seemed just as determined to keep him in her arms. "You were pretty funny back there with that big owl chasing you."

"That was no owl, I told you," said Tyler.

"Tyler, I saw it with my own two eyes. It was an owl," she said. She looked down at Jasper and winked. They had reached the wrought iron fence, Jasper noted with some relief. The girl would surely have to put him down now.

"Here," she held Jasper out for Tyler to take.

Tyler looked at her. "What?"

"You hold him while I go over, then you hand him to me through the fence, then you come over," she said.

"No way," Tyler said. "I'm not holding some mangy graveyard cat."

Good boy, Jasper thought as he squirmed hard to twist out of Brittany's grip and dropped to the ground. He hurried a few steps away and stopped.

"Tyler!" she said. "You let him get away." She reached for Jasper but he avoided her grasp.

"So what?" Tyler said as he gripped the fence and began to climb.

Brittany stood and looked at Jasper. "Come on, Lucky."

Lucky? Jasper thought. *Now there's the name for me.* He slipped through the iron spikes and sat down. The girl started her climb. The other boy, Ames, reached the fence white-faced and breathless as they were ready to walk away, so they waited for him to scramble over.

There wasn't much talking on the way home. Jasper trailed the girl from a comfortable few feet and she kept looking back to make sure that he was there. They were all limping with fatigue when they reached the street where the girl lived.

"Bye, Brittany. I'm sorry about trying to scare you." Tyler's whisper sounded contrite.

"Bye, Brittany. I'm sorry too," Ames said.

"'S'okay," she said. "See you." She looked at Jasper. "Come on, Lucky."

Jasper scanned the yard for any signs of the gray and black cats. Brittany walked to a tree in the front yard with branches like great outstretched arms and swung herself up, nimble as a monkey. He watched as she climbed one massive branch to an open window and slipped inside. She stuck her head out the window and called to him in a fierce whisper.

"Lucky!" she said. "Come here."

It was his dream, beckoning from the window. Loving caresses, a warm soft bed, and a bowl refilled with food every day. So why then did he hesitate?

He looked around for Hank.

"I'm here," Hank said, from the open-armed tree, perched on one of the higher thick branches.

"You did a wonderful job back there," said Jasper as he picked his way up the tree. "Thanks for your help."

"Are you going inside?" Hank said. "What if she won't let you back out?"

"Do I look like an indoor cat to you?" said Jasper.

"I don't know. What does an indoor cat look like?" Hank said.

Jasper paused near the window while the girl whispered and stretched toward him.

"I'll show you tomorrow," he said, as he walked into Brittany's eager hands. She pulled him inside and hugged him close.

"You're my Lucky charm cat," she said. "You're magic. Alicia sent you, I know."

A little shiver went down Jasper's spine. *What's she talking about? Who is this Alicia?*

She dropped him gently on a tousled bed covered with a vivid orange and green bedspread. He crouched and took a series of short, quick breaths, tasting the smells of grape bubble gum and paper and the powdery, sweet smell of the girl. She pulled the screen back in place with practiced ease.

Brittany shrugged off her clothes and pulled on a tie-dyed tee shirt that hung below the knobs of her knees. She hopped back on the bed and pulled the covers up.

"Lucky," she whispered. "Come here."

Jasper picked his way through the jumble of sheet and blanket and bedspread to sit by her head. He sniffed at her face and gently licked her eyelid.

"Oooh." She pulled away. "You've got a scratchy tongue."

He moved to the top of the pillow and reclined. He sniffed at her hair. It smelled nice, grass-fresh and faintly musky. He chewed on a few strands to test the flavor.

"Lucky!" Brittany hunched down in the bed. "You're eating my hair. Stop."

He moved down the bed to lie beside her and curled up against her back. She took a deep breath and then another. Jasper closed his eyes.

Chapter 8

UNLIGHT SPILLED INTO THE ROOM with the low buzz of lawnmowers and the rumble of voices in the rest of the house. Jasper stood up and hopped off the bed to take a look around.

The room was cluttered with books and balls, clothes and stuffed animals. Big colorful pictures of people covered the walls. Probably friends of the girl, maybe family.

One thing looked like it didn't belong. A small white table, edged with a filmy fabric that hung from the edge to the floor, stood in one corner like a prim lonely altar. A mirror hung on the wall just above the table; a narrow satin-topped bench was pushed neatly underneath. On top of the table sat a framed photograph, a tiny ivory cat, and a ceramic lamp, with a base shaped like a twirling ballerina. A pair of small soft dancing shoes were placed precisely in the center, the ribbon laces straight and aligned.

"Are you awake?" Brittany lay on her side, head propped on her elbow.

Footsteps clicked down the hall and stopped just outside. The door opened.

"Brittany, get up. It's time for breakfast," said a tall woman with one hand on the doorknob. She disappeared from the door, still talking. "Hurry up now. I need your help with Nathan. Cole's got a regional semi-final in Columbia and we've got to be on the road in half an hour."

Jasper jumped back on the bed. Brittany pulled the covers up tight around her and sighed so hard the bed quivered. Jasper stretched and started toward the window.

More footsteps down the hall, softer this time. Another face appeared in the door: two round eyes in a small squashed face peered into the room. The eyes widened. It was the small boy who had been with Brittany in the woods.

"Kitty!" The boy with the odd face ran flat-footed to the side of the bed. Jasper shrank back a little. The boy's sudden jerky movements were just as unnerving as Jasper remembered.

"Easy, Nathan, just move slowly and let him sniff your hand," Brittany said, sitting up. "Give him a chance to remember you."

"Kitty, kitty," the boy crooned as he sat on the bed and carefully extended a hand to Jasper. Jasper took a delicate sniff and smelled a roasted, grainy smell, like popcorn. He rubbed his head against Nathan's fingers and the boy smiled like a blooming flower. He patted Jasper's head gently, with an open palm.

"Good kitty," he said, jumbled and quick.

"He is a good kitty," Brittany said. "His name is Lucky."

"Wucky," the boy repeated.

Quick purposeful footsteps clicked in the hall then the tall woman was standing in the doorway again.

"Brittany Madeline Rogers," she said. "What did I tell you about bringing those stray cats inside?"

"He's not a stray," Brittany said. "He's magic."

The woman laughed, a short dry cough. "Magic?" She moved to stand close to the boy and reached out to stroke his head. "That's good news. I could use a little magic."

Brittany rolled her eyes. The boy continued to pat Jasper with a careful flat hand. The woman studied Jasper a long hard moment, then walked to the window and opened the blinds. Jasper closed his eyes and felt the swell of hope in his chest. *So she didn't throw you out at first look. It doesn't mean she'll let you stay.*

"How is he magic, sweetie?" Her voice was softer. Her eyes went to the white table in the corner of the room. Frustration flashed on her face, then a look of deep fatigue.

"Magic, magic," the boy said, bouncing the bed a little. Jasper stiffened to keep his balance and started moving toward Brittany.

Brittany shrugged. "Don't bounce the bed, Nathan."

The tall woman circled the bed and extended her fingers for Jasper to sniff. The woman smelled like flowers and bacon and a faint chemical smell he couldn't identify. He rubbed himself against her hand with abandon, thinking of the bacon.

"Well, he's certainly friendly enough." The woman touched his head with her fingertips. "Is that what makes him magic?"

"Magic, magic," the boy chanted, jumped from the bed and ran to the white table. Jasper hopped to the floor.

"No," Brittany said. "Nathan, get away from there. Mom, make him stop."

"Nathan," the woman said.

Nathan plucked one of the ballet shoes from the top of the table and held it to his cheek.

"Nathan!" Brittany said. "Mom!"

"Calm down, Brittany," the woman said. "He's not hurting anything."

"He'll get it all dirty. He's not supposed to touch it." Brittany's face was red and contorted.

"Honey, it's just a shoe." The tall woman moved to stand behind Nathan and hugged him while he cocked his head and rubbed the satin shoe against his cheek.

"It is not!" Brittany threw the sheets and comforter off and lunged toward the boy. She clutched the shoe and Nathan twisted away from her.

"Let go!" she said.

"Brittany." The tall woman put a hand on Brittany's shoulder. "Just calm down. I'm sure Nathan will give it to you if you ask him nicely."

Brittany yanked the shoe away from Nathan. "I told you to leave it alone. Why don't you understand?"

Nathan turned and ran from the room. The flat thumping of his feet down the stairs echoed in the suddenly quiet room.

The woman put her hands on her hips. "Are you happy now?"

Brittany shrugged and placed the ballet shoe back on the table so that it was precisely aligned with the other. "He knows he's not supposed to touch Alicia's things."

The tall woman stared at the white table then at the girl. "You know, it might be time to put the table away."

"No!" Brittany's head shot up. She stood between the table and her mother. "I won't let you."

The woman sighed and walked to the closet. "We need to get going. Brittany, I need for you to get dressed and ready to go."

"I don't want to go to Columbia," Brittany said. She moved to the edge of the bed and sat, her legs dangling to the floor.

"I think your denim skirt would look nice. How about this top?" The woman held out a crisp green blouse.

Brittany reached for Jasper and cradled him in her arms. "How about if I stay with Tyler today? His mom won't mind."

"If you don't go, who will sit with Nathan?" The woman flipped through the hanging clothes.

"You?" Brittany said. "Or Dad?"

The woman sighed and turned back toward the bed. "You know Daddy's the coach and I'm responsible for refreshments. Of course I'll sit with you both, but I need your help. Please don't be selfish today."

Brittany stroked Jasper, her head down, her hair a thin silky curtain around her face.

The woman stared hard at Jasper. She frowned and wrinkled

her nose. "Honey, where did you find that cat? He's a little rough around the edges, don't you think?"

The hope that had been growing in Jasper's chest like a buoyant small bubble popped.

Brittany stiffened and pulled him close. "He's beautiful. I told you, he's magic. He's not like other cats."

The woman turned and started toward the door. "You did say he was magic and you can tell me why on the ride down to Columbia. This is a big match for Cole. I know you want to be there to cheer for him. It means a lot to him that you're there."

Brittany lifted her head and spoke to her mother's back. "He doesn't care if I'm there or not. And it embarrasses him to bring Nathan."

The woman whirled and took two long steps to the bed. She brought her face close to the girl's and spoke in a low, fierce voice. "Don't you ever let me hear you say that again. Cole loves Nathan. Nobody in this family is ashamed of anybody and for you to say so is cruel and mean-spirited. Is that what you want to be? Cruel and mean-spirited?"

Brittany lowered her head again and began rocking gently.

The woman straightened up and glanced at her wristwatch.

"Get out of that bed and get dressed. Put that cat outside."

Brittany didn't move.

"Now, Brittany." The woman's voice was hard and unyielding. "Put that cat out now."

"I'll do it as soon as I get dressed." Her body felt stiff as a young sapling to Jasper.

"Now, Brittany." The woman wasn't backing down.

"You want me to go outside in this?" Brittany pinched her streaky tee shirt in mock dismay.

The woman took a step and plucked Jasper out of the girl's arms. She turned and stalked from the room.

"Lucky!" Brittany wailed.

"Wucky!" Nathan cried from down the hall.

The woman held Jasper carefully away from her body, as if he were a small can of dripping garbage. They went down a series of steps then walked into a room that smelled like it had to be the kitchen. She set him on the floor with one hand clamped down around his shoulders as if he might try to bolt back up the stairs.

She opened the door and scooted him with her foot. He walked outside, tail high and quirking with pride. He'd spent the night inside.

The air smelled of dew-kissed earth and the dry baked breath of summer. Jasper blinked in the sudden spill of light. For a moment, he couldn't see, so he tasted the air and felt the swell of it in his chest. Everything looked different.

He found a spot in the morning sun and felt her gaze grow more intense. For once, it felt like the sun was smiling at him, watching him, focusing on him with the loving eye of a mother, or maybe a favorite aunt. Maybe that was the connection: the sun was sister to the moon. He squinted at the sky and the sun smiled a fierce and silent salutation.

———

Jasper waited in the yard until Brittany, wearing purple shorts and a tee shirt, burst out of the house, Nathan close behind. Jasper trotted up to meet her. She knelt down in the grass and hugged him. The boy reached in for a few flat-handed pats.

"Don't worry. I'll be back this afternoon. Are you hungry?" She searched his eyes.

He gave her a loving, hungry look. She jumped up and ran back into the house. In minutes, she ran back out balancing a bowl of water and a saucer piled high with wet, sticky food. She set the dishes in front of Jasper.

"There you go, boy. Hope it's good."

"Good!" the boy said. He reached out for the food and Brittany pushed him away.

"That's cat food, Nathan. You wouldn't like it."

"Let's go." The woman stood in the doorway. "Brittany, I need your help with this cooler, please."

Jasper finished the meal before they were out of the driveway. He tried to slow down and enjoy it, but kept looking over his shoulder for the gray and black cats. He licked the plate clean and lapped a healthy dose of water from the bowl. His stomach felt too full for travel so he settled under the bushes shaded by a big oak tree for a nap.

Dozing in the bushes, he heard voices. The wind was wafting his way and he could smell cats — he strained to listen more closely while he squinted through the leaves.

They were sniffing around his breakfast saucer.

"We missed it, Chloe," the black cat said. "How did we miss it?"

The gray cat sat, scanning the yard for him, Jasper was convinced.

"She's feeding somebody else." Chloe flexed her claws.

"Who?" said the black cat.

"That blotchy beat-up thing."

"What blotchy beat-up thing?" The black cat licked the saucer.

"Joey! You know! That sorry excuse for a cat that we ran out of the yard yesterday." Chloe bristled a little at the thought.

Joey shook his head. "You were the one that chased him out of the yard. He didn't seem so bad to me."

"Nobody seems bad to you. That's your problem. You like everybody." The gray cat kept looking and scenting the air.

"And what's wrong with that?" He licked her head. "I like you."

She sniffed, blinked, and unclenched her claws. "Everybody likes me. I can't help it if I'm irresistible."

"Irresistible and ill-tempered." He gave her a slow sweet eye kiss.

She batted softly at his ear and they tumbled in a joyful silent skirmish.

Jasper watched, and felt something sore and oddly hollow in the center of his chest. He remembered wrestling with his brothers and sisters, the playful camaraderie. There was nothing quite like the company of cats. The comfort of a warm furry body pressed against your back, the feel of a warm tongue on your head. The space inside him ached.

The grappling cats tumbled closer, until Chloe darted into the bushes for a reprieve. She stood, breathing hard, until she looked around her.

"I knew it!" she said with grim satisfaction. "I knew you were somewhere around." Her tail became a thick brushy rope as she turned sideways to him and shifted herself into the horseshoe shape of the cat at war.

"I'm just sitting here," he said. "Not bothering anybody."

"You're bothering me," she hissed.

Joey poked his head through the bushes. "What's going on?"

"She's getting ready to try and kill me again," Jasper said.

"Chloe!" Joey walked up to Jasper and sniffed eagerly of him. "Just take it easy. He seems like an okay cat."

"He's ugly!" she said. "And homeless! A thief! Can't you see what he's trying to do with Brittany?"

Joey thought for a moment and studied Jasper. "What are you trying to do with Brittany?"

"He's trying to steal her, you idiot! Don't you see?" Chloe's eyes sparked fire and her tail whipped back and forth. "Get out of the way, Joey."

"Is that true?" asked Joey.

"No," said Jasper. "She just seems to like me. If she belongs to you, isn't there room for one more? She seems to think so."

"She has no sense. She's a person." Chloe crouched.

"She has a point, you know." Joey looked at Jasper. "Brittany has no understanding of these things. She's just a person."

"But isn't it Brittany's choice?" The voice came from above, and when Jasper looked up, he saw the bulky outline of Hank perched on a leafy branch.

Joey and Chloe dropped low to the ground and froze.

"Hello, Hank," said Jasper.

"Hi, Jasper," Hank said. "Who are your friends?"

Jasper smiled to himself. "This black cat is Joey, and that's Chloe." The two cats hugged the ground, barely breathing.

"Hello," Hank called out.

"Don't be afraid," Jasper said. "Hank's a fine fellow. He won't hurt you."

"That's an owl," Joey said in a gasping whisper. "A great horned owl. He could take your head off!"

"I don't think so," said Hank. "Jasper has quite a large head for his body. See how thick his neck is?"

Chloe quivered like a plump gray raindrop.

"Hank!" Jasper said. "You're scaring them."

"Scaring them? I'm so sorry," said Hank. "I would never hurt a cat, thick neck or skinny."

"How can we be sure of that?" Joey asked.

Hank shrugged and blinked one of his slow deliberate blinks that reminded Jasper of a door opening and closing. "You can't. But I haven't hurt Jasper."

Joey and Chloe looked at each other and whispered.

"How was your night inside?" Hank spoke to Jasper.

"Inside?" Chloe began to puff up again. "She took you inside?"

"It's really nothing," Jasper groomed a spot on his shoulder.

"She kept you inside the whole night?" asked Joey.

Jasper nodded. Joey and Chloe exchanged a look.

"Well, it's more than nothing to me." Joey stood up, keeping one eye on Hank. "Feeding you is one thing, but taking you inside for the whole night is another."

"I can't help it," Jasper said. "She likes me. She wants me inside. What am I supposed to do, run away?"

"Yes," Chloe hissed. "Run away and never come back."

"That's not very nice," Hank said. Joey and Chloe's heads jerked at the sound of his voice and they both crouched down again.

Jasper shook his head. "I still don't see how it hurts you two for Brittany to like me."

"You just don't get it." The tip of Chloe's tail began to wiggle back and forth.

"You don't know Brittany," Joey said. "How she is."

Jasper and Hank waited.

"At first, you're everything." Joey studied the ground. "She'll be all excited over you and you're the special one." He looked at Chloe. "Or ones."

"Then?" Hank said.

Joey and Chloe stared at Hank.

"And then what happens?" Hank adjusted his grip on the branch and one loose leaf fluttered off the limb. All three cats watched the leaf drift to the ground.

"Then she gets bored," Joey said. "And if you make one little mistake, you're not so special anymore. The problem is," he swallowed hard, "her dad has already threatened to take us to the animal shelter. Brittany may have to make a choice: two outdoor cats or one indoor cat."

Hank was quiet and Jasper could imagine the thoughts he was picking up from Joey and Chloe. The two of them nuzzled and huddled close. They were such beautiful cats: Joey, all black and lean and sinewy, like a miniature panther with a broad kind face and Chloe, plump and glossy, with small delicate feet and her prissy, vicious ways.

Jasper's leg ached a little as he watched them. He scratched his ear and felt his own dry, coarse coat. It prickled all over and it seemed like he could feel the roughness seeping under his skin, working into the center of him.

The girl wants me. She thinks I'm special. What's wrong with that? Why shouldn't I be the chosen one for once? Those two are beautiful and appealing, they'd have no trouble finding another home. Why should I have to worry about what happens to them?

"Jasper," Hank said. "Why don't we go back to the fort?"

"No."

He looked at Hank and his deep round eyes and he felt the weight of the moon's judgment. She would not be pleased.

Of course she won't be pleased. She always wants me to do the most difficult and uncomfortable thing. When you got right down to it, she hasn't really helped me much at all.

"I'm waiting for the girl to come back," said Jasper.

Chloe looked at him with hatred and desperation, then ran through the bushes like something was chasing her. Joey sighed and turned to face Jasper.

"Hope she doesn't get tired of you too," he said. He loped away.

There was a strained silence. Jasper tried to curl up and relax but the comforting feel of the morning had passed.

"Jasper," said Hank. "Do you think you're doing the right thing?"

Jasper closed his eyes and pretended to be asleep.

Chapter 9

SHADOWS STRETCHED and the air cooled again, like the earth was exhaling in relief that another day was over. Jasper sat in the bushes, dozing, remembering the smooth feel of the sheets against his fur. The soft springiness of the girl's bed. The supreme comfort of a full belly. Thinking of those things helped him ignore the faint wrong feeling in his chest and at the back of his head.

He sat and dozed and groomed himself. He thought about Brittany and wondered how the day had gone for her. And then, without warning, he thought about his brown-eyed boy. His boy that moved away. *Where is he? Did he find another cat? Does he ever think about me?*

What felt like a heavy shadow in his chest dissolved into an aching throb of something else, that old sore feeling that made him whimper like a kitten. He shook his head and tried to make his mind completely blank and peaceful. Then a new thought struck him like a bee sting. The mind pictures always came to him whether he wanted them or not. Random as the weather. Why couldn't he pick the situation that he wanted to see?

Of course! He thought and jumped to his feet with excitement. *Why not? What could it hurt?*

He took a quick look around to make sure he was alone then settled down in the bushes again. He lowered himself and sat, paws stretched in front of him like a sphinx. Closed his eyes and thought of the boy's face. His image of the face was blurry, indistinct, and faded into the backlit dimness of what he saw when he closed his eyes.

Jasper shook his head and tried again, letting the boy's face stay vague and elusive, just thinking of the warmth of his hands and the hum of his voice and the unspeakable comfort of his company.

And then it happened. He saw the boy sitting on a log in a clearing in the middle of a forest. Clearly, it was cooler weather wherever the boy had gone. The trees were stark and naked of leaves. The boy wore a coat and gloves and shivered, hunched against the wind, with one hand in his pocket and one hand holding a leash. Jasper didn't want to, but he made himself look at the end of the leash.

It was a dog. A small chocolate Lab, a puppy, but nevertheless a dog. Jasper's heart dropped and rolled like a discarded ball. He watched as the boy lifted the brown puppy. Wriggling and squirming, the puppy aimed wild licks at the boy's face. The boy laughed and Jasper felt the sound of it echo inside his chest like the slamming of a door.

Jasper opened his eyes and stood. The yard was still quiet, only the birds spoke among themselves as always. And one bird spoke to Jasper.

"Who's the boy?" Hank asked from a low branch of the closest tree.

Jasper looked up. "Someone I used to know."

"A friend?" Hank said.

Jasper shrugged and stretched. "Used to be."

"I'm confused." Hank shifted his weight.

Jasper said nothing and curled himself down under the shrubs again.

"Why does it upset you that he's happy?" Hank's words splashed him like a blast from a garden hose.

"You don't understand," Jasper sat up again.

"Explain it to me," Hank said.

"He used to be mine," Jasper stared at the empty driveway. "He used to pet me and feed me."

"Like Brittany?" Hank asked.

Jasper nodded. "Then he went away. His family left and he had to go with them."

Hank blinked slowly. "And he's somewhere else now, with a puppy."

"Yes," Jasper said, very softly.

Hank was quiet for a long moment. "So that's how Chloe and Joey feel."

The thought jarred him. "No," Jasper said. "That's different."

Hank cocked his head. "You're right. Brittany didn't go away, she's still right here. And instead of a puppy, she's found you."

"But that's not my fault!" Jasper said, his tail whipping in frustration.

"Not the puppy's fault either, is it?" Hank said. He stared out over the yard and shook his head. "You know what I don't understand?"

Jasper sat in sullen silence.

"Why are those humans so important to you? Why do you care if they pay any attention to you or not?"

Jasper gave a tremendous sigh as a car pulled into the driveway. "I'll explain it to you later."

The car was the one that Brittany had left in that morning. Brittany and Nathan spilled out of the doors when it stopped. A man and an older boy remained in the car, the man talking and gesturing, the boy staring straight ahead.

Brittany ran to the middle of the yard.

"Lucky!" she said. Jasper trotted up to meet her. She sat down in the grass and hugged him. "I'm so glad you're here. I was afraid you might go away." She kissed his head. "What have you been doing all day?"

"Brittany!" The mother called from behind the car. "Come get this cooler, please."

Brittany sighed and slowly rose.

"Now that may be the ugliest cat I've ever seen." The man stood in the driveway and stared at Jasper. "Lord, Brittany, where'd you get that one, from a dumpster?"

Jasper kept his eyes on Brittany and told himself that it didn't matter what anybody else said or thought.

The older boy snickered. "Yeah, good job. Who needs a watchdog when you've got a cat so ugly he scares people away?"

The man snorted and opened the trunk of his car. The woman saw Brittany's crumpling face. "Oh, you guys don't know anything. That cat's got something better than good looks."

Jasper's heart lifted, just a little.

"Oh yeah?" the boy said. "Like what? A smell worse that a skunk?"

"That's enough, Cole," the woman said. "Speaking of smells, I need for you to take a shower before dinner. Nathan, I think you can carry this bag. Let's go, guys."

They drifted inside and Jasper sat outside in the deepening shadows. The sky darkened, the moon glowed, and it seemed like the smudges on her face were darker and more pronounced. Thin, sheer clouds drifted across her face and she was silent, preoccupied.

He avoided looking directly at her; he focused on the house, the lighted windows, the dim murmur of voices, scraping chairs, tinkles of dishes and silverware that told him they were eating dinner. And the smells: the rich luscious smells of roasting meat and warm bread and maybe macaroni and cheese.

Jasper concentrated so hard on the door to the house that he barely noticed as the moon drifted higher in the sky. He thought he heard a faint hooting from close by but he kept staring at the door as if to will the girl to open it and beckon him in.

She did come back, with a pan of dry food and fresh water. She petted and stroked him while he ate and picked him up when he slowed his bites.

"Joey!" she called. "Chloe!"

The two cats slipped from the shadows like they had been waiting. With a baleful glance at Jasper, Chloe crouched in front of the pan and sniffed at the food. Joey ambled up and started crunching without a word to Jasper.

"I can't bring you inside again right now, Lucky," Brittany said as she cradled him in her arms and rubbed his head. "I have to give you a bath first. Tomorrow, okay?"

Jasper closed his eyes and purred. The baths his mother had given him were lovely: warm tongue scrubbings.

"Ha!" said Chloe, between delicate bites. "Mr. Favorite Cat of the Week gets a bath!"

"Lucky him," said Joey, with a full mouth and a smirk.

They're just jealous, Jasper thought. *Obviously their mothers mistreated them.*

After she put him down and Chloe and Joey scattered away like they didn't want to get too close to him, he slept in the bushes again, away from any trees and the knowing gaze of the cloud-spotted moon. His sleep was fitful, disturbed. Unaccustomed to sleeping on the ground, he tensed at the slightest noise. A dog started barking and he jumped up so fast he scraped his back on the low-growing shrub branches. As he tried to settle back to sleep, he felt that knot of dread deep in his belly that always seemed to precede one of his unbidden mind pictures. He clenched his eyes shut, covered his nose with his tail, and thought fierce deliberate thoughts of the frosty-haired woman.

The images took recognizable shape and movement inexorably, despite his resistance. It was Chloe being stalked by a dog. A lean, big-footed Doberman, taking springy, unhurried strides across the grass. The most terrible thing about the vision was that Chloe didn't see or hear the dog coming. She was mincing through the yard, chasing a bird. Jasper winced.

Why did this have to happen now? Where did these pictures come from? What could I do to make them stop? He was tired of taking care of everybody else. Why didn't somebody have a mind picture about him – the countless hungry and cold nights he'd had, or the bad experiences with the Chow and the Chevy Malibu? Who had ever rescued him?

"I would rescue you," said Hank from the roof.

Jasper jerked at the sound of his voice.

"Sorry," said Hank. "I know that dog."

Jasper sank back to the ground. "Of course you do."

"He lives two streets over from the big angry man. The man's dog knows him."

Max, Jasper thought.

"Max," said Hank. "Is that his name?"

"Don't you remember?" Jasper stopped. Hank wouldn't remember; he'd been asleep while Jasper and the dog had talked. "Max is the big angry man's dog."

Hank shook his head. "I just remember him leading the man right to us in the tree and then—" He shuddered.

"I know," said Jasper. "But I talked to him after we helped them out of the house and he said he wouldn't try to kill us anymore."

"I didn't help them out of the house." Hank looked up at the sky. "That was you, Jasper."

Jasper couldn't think of anything to say. A pleasantly warm feeling settled in his chest and oozed like honey up to his head and down into his belly. It was true – he was the one that helped them out of the house. Then he shook his head. He couldn't leave Brittany's house. *I need to be there when she comes out in the morning.*

"She'll wait for you," Hank said.

"How do you know that?" Jasper said, as he stood up and began pacing. "How do you know she won't think I'm just some unfaithful stray who's not interested in a real home?"

Hank thought for a long moment. "If you had a real home with

Brittany like you want, would you never come outside?"

"Of course I would come outside," Jasper said. He took a deep breath of the vibrant night air and looked up. The moon nodded at him, the clouds gone.

"Would you ever leave the yard?" Hank said.

"Of course I would leave the yard!" Jasper said. "I couldn't stay in one yard for the rest of my life!"

"So, let's say right now you have a real home with Brittany." Hank shifted his weight and blinked. "You're outside, and you can leave the yard. So why can't you go with me to talk to the angry man's dog?"

"Max," Jasper said.

"Maybe Max could help us out with the Doberman," Hank said.

"But I don't want to!" Jasper said and he sat down. "I don't even like Chloe. She's been mean to me and maybe she needs to get chased a little. And I told you, I don't want to risk anything with Brittany."

The wind picked up and pushed through the trees with a dulled hiss. A dog barked suddenly, harshly somewhere in the distance. The cat and the owl considered each other in the cool folds of light and shadow.

Hank looked over his head. "I'm beginning to think this business of having a home is a terrible thing."

"Terrible?" Jasper stood up again. "What's terrible about it? It's the best thing in the world!"

Hank shook his head. "Not from where I stand." He stretched out his wings and took off into the night.

"Hank!" Jasper cried and listened to the weak sound of his voice in the shadowy stillness. He tried once more. "Hank!"

———

Jasper got to the angry man's house as the moon was fading in the sky and the first blush of the sun was announcing her arrival. The dog was already outside and staring up into the limbs of a sugar maple in the angry man's back yard. Despite his last conversation with the dog, Jasper felt a fluttery gust of fear in his chest. He licked his lips, mouth suddenly dry. He approached the dog as quickly and quietly as he could.

"—cat named Chloe. You know the one." Jasper recognized Hank's voice. "You always see her with the black cat. She lives a few blocks over with the girl named Brittany."

The dog cocked his head. "I think I know who you're talking about. Gray, kind of fat?"

"That's the one." Hank said. "Then you'll talk to the Doberman."

"Me?" The dog laughed, a short harsh bark. "Brutus is bigger, meaner, and younger than me. How am I supposed to talk him out of his fun?"

"A smart dog like you," Jasper said. "You could think of something."

The dog whirled to face Jasper and yipped in surprise. "Huh? What is it with you two? You're giving me the creeps!"

"Just a simple favor, Max." Jasper sat down. "There's a cat that could get in a bad spot with that Dobie unless you can help us out. Couldn't you talk to him?"

"Like I told Mr. Big Eyes here, I don't think having a heart to heart with Brutus is going to do much good." Max sniffed around the yard. "Damn poodle's been over here again. I'd like to catch that sissy French-fry just once."

"Fine." Jasper looked up at Hank. "Well, Hank, I guess we've done all we can do. We can't be responsible for the consequences." He stood and turned to go.

"Hold on a minute." Max took a few steps toward them. "What do you mean by consequences?"

Hank looked at Jasper, eyes wide and confused.

"Oh nothing," Jasper said. "Just that we try to keep an eye out for everybody, unless somebody doesn't do his part, then he's disqualified."

"Disqualified?" Max said, his voice high and thin.

Hank blinked. "You have to do what you can when you can."

Jasper nodded. "That's it." He started to trot away. "Let's see if we can find Chloe, Hank. Maybe she'll listen to us."

"Wait a minute, don't be in so much of a hurry. You guys are moving too fast for me." Max followed Jasper. "I never said I wanted to be disqualified."

Jasper stopped again, so abruptly that Max almost walked onto him. Max jumped back, muttering an apology.

"Well, nobody wants to be disqualified, Max," Jasper said. "It's just what happens. You don't help; you don't get any more warnings or help. It's as simple as that. Right, Hank?"

Hank had flown to the lowest branch of an oak tree above them. "That's right, Jasper."

"It may seem harsh, but just think, Max, what would happen if we went around helping everybody and they didn't help back?" Jasper looked the dog in the eye. "What would be the point?"

Max sat and scratched his belly reflectively. "See what you mean there. Well, I can't make any promises, but I'll do the best I can."

"Great," said Jasper.

Max got up and started to trot toward his doghouse. "Now this means I'm still in, right? Not disqualified."

"You've got to do the best you can," said Hank. "No matter what."

"That's right," said Jasper. "No half efforts."

"Okay, okay," said Max. "I hear you."

A door creaked open and Jasper could see the big man in his doorway, newspaper rolled in his hand. He whistled for Max. The dog took off at a lope.

"What are you doing out there?" The big angry man's voice echoed in the quiet morning. "What are you doing letting that cat just sit there in my yard like he owned it?" There was a smacking sound as he whacked the side of the house above Max's head with the paper. Max ducked a little but kept smiling, tail swinging. He pushed his head into the man's leg.

"You know better than that. You know what to do with cats. You getting lazy or something?" The man roughly fondled the dog's head.

"Did I hear an owl out there?" The man straightened and squinted toward the two of them. "Wonder if it's that same one that woke us up the night of the fire."

The man looked down at Max. "You know, that bird may have saved our lives."

Jasper and Hank looked at each other and smiled.

Chapter 10

ORNING DAWNED WARM AND HUMID, the
sun stretching and flexing in the faded blue sky like she
was boasting about wearing the color out of it. After
the visit to Max, Jasper had returned to Brittany's yard
and slept the restful sleep of the righteous until the radiant eye of the
sun fell upon him and he heard Brittany's voice.

"Lucky!" She leaped off the back steps, balancing two bowls. He
twined himself around her legs and meowed his pleasure to see her,
to have food, to be alive on such a glorious day. The sharp, accusing
triangle faces of Chloe and Joey peeking at him from the bushes bothered him not a hair. He was the cat of honor, the favorite cat, the cat
that really mattered.

He ate with the delicacy and care befitting a well-loved cat who
knows his next meal is coming soon, before he gets hungry to the tips
of his claws. He took reasonable mouthfuls and stopped briefly
between bites to look around and enjoy the yard, the grass, the smell
of bacon wafting through the air, the sound of voices from the house,
the sense that he belonged here. Finally he finished and he groomed

himself with particular care, watching Chloe and Joey eat and glare from their pan on the other side of the yard.

Brittany dragged a big round open box out in the grass. She pulled the hose into the box and soon the sound of water splashing was too much to resist. Jasper walked over for a closer look while she went back into the house.

The round box was too tall for him to look into; it had the hard, cold feel of the fast-moving heavy cars that brought humans home and took them away. He hopped his front paws up against the side to try to get his head high enough to take a look. The sound of splashing water fascinated him; he'd had wonderful playful meals by creeks more than once. Frogs, tadpoles, tiny flashing minnows, he shivered with the fun of it.

Brittany came back out of the house, her arms and legs long and bare, looking more than ever like a giant pale spider. She wore floppy shoes that slapped her feet as she walked and carried a bottle and an armful of towels. Jasper lifted his tail and sang out.

"Brittany's building a little pond!" It wasn't every human who would be so thoughtful and creative as to make a tiny pond where the favorite cat could play.

"A pond?" Chloe flicked up just the tip of her tail where she lay in the shade of the bushes. "Oh goody. Look, Joey, it's a pond!"

Then she and Joey shared a laugh; nasty sneering snickers that gave Jasper a quivery little question down deep in his gut. He chose to ignore it.

Jealousy, he thought. *Such an ugly cat habit. Why can't they be happy for me?*

"Come here, Lucky." Brittany bent to pick him up and he went limp and boneless. He lay in her arms on his back, legs splayed, blinking up at her sweet face. Then she turned him over quickly. Too quickly for him to react. She hopped into the tiny pond. Down he went, into the awful drenching wetness of it.

He wasn't underwater, but he couldn't breathe for the shock. His limbs went stiff. He howled.

"It's okay, Lucky," she said as she held him down and wiped his head with a wet cloth.

It was definitely not okay. He was in shock. His fur was completely soaked. His skin was in danger of melting away.

"You're such a good boy," she crooned. Then she picked up the bottle and poured some awful gooey liquid on him. She rubbed him and the goo became a bigger foamy mess that she seemed intent in spreading all over him.

He cried out again and thought he heard laughter. *The fiends. They had known.*

"Jasper?" It was Hank, bless him. "Jasper, are you all right?"

"No!" he sobbed. "I'm not all right."

"What's she doing to you?" Hank sounded worried.

The laughter grew louder. "It's called a bath, Lucky boy! Isn't it wonderful?" It sounded like Chloe.

"I'm sorry, sweetie," Brittany said to him. "I know you hate this. It's just that Mom says you have to have a bath if you're going to come inside."

The thought of going inside seemed vague and distant. All he wanted was to get out of this terrible, cold pool of water. Everything was wet; legs, tail, belly, fur dead-heavy and matted like skin that didn't fit. Once he fell into the creek by accident and drenched his legs and belly but it had never been this bad. He struggled and tried to get a foothold to scramble up the sides of the pond but the sides were as slick inside as out, and his friend Brittany was doing her best to hold him in the awful chilling stuff and keep rubbing the nasty goo-foam over every part of him. *How long was this going to go on?*

"Jasper?" Hank called out again. "Want me to help? Fly by and try to scare her?"

The thought of scaring Brittany was not a good one. This was torture but she had done so many good things for him. He was torn.

"Jasper?" Hank persisted. "Maybe I can distract her."

"Maybe I can distract her," Joey rolled out of the bushes, weak with laughter. "I don't think one bath is going to do it. He's so filthy, he'll need two every day."

"Put some more of that gooey stuff on him, Brittany." Chloe's voice drifted from the shrubs and the venom settled deep in Jasper's bones. "He needs it on his face."

He squeezed his eyes shut and tried to block the voices and the wetness and the gooey foam out of his mind. *They were savages. Blind, selfish savages who thought only of themselves. This awful thing will be over soon. It will be over and I will be dry again, sitting in the sun, feeling the soft light comfort that is my fur against my skin. I'll be eating canned food. Chasing a squirrel. Catching it.*

"What a sweet, wonderful, beautiful boy you are," Brittany whispered. She rinsed the foam from his coat and finally lifted him from the cursed bath pond.

He shivered, feeling skinny and exposed, cold to his bones, thoroughly humiliated. She wrapped him in a thick towel and tried to hold him but he squirmed and twisted free. He dashed to the far end of the bushes, away from the other two, and shook himself hard. He crouched and shivered and began to groom himself. *Where to begin?*

"Just look at him, Joey." Chloe's eyes gleamed from a few shrubs away. "Look at Mr. Indoor Cat now. All wet and nasty."

"Pretty pathetic," Joey sat behind her. "Nothing sadder than an ugly wet cat."

Jasper licked his back leg in short little strokes and tried to ignore them.

"Lucky!" Brittany stood in the grass by the bath pond with the towel in her hands.

"You realize, of course," said Chloe, "that baths are a regular thing for indoor cats."

Jasper licked steadily on. Brittany walked toward the bushes where he sat.

"Did you get water in your ears, Mangy?" Chloe said. "I'm talking to you." She edged closer, sniffed and grimaced. "Smell him, Joey. He smells like that stuff they spray on the grass to kill the weeds."

Something in Jasper's head snapped. Claws out, his paw swiped at her smirking face.

She yowled. Her ears flattened and her eyes flashed. "Ooooooh, Mr. Mangy wants to tangle."

"Lucky?" Brittany parted the bushes and peered in. "Chloe, what are you doing? Leave him alone."

Chloe's tail whipped back and forth.

He started to lick his shoulder. "You heard her. Get lost."

"This is not your yard, Mangy." Chloe crouched.

Jasper blinked at her. "Wake up, Chubbo. Have you checked with Brittany about that lately?"

Brittany reached in to pick Jasper up. Chloe struck at him. The claws intended for him raked the girl's hand instead.

"Ow!" Brittany jerked her hand back and stomped. "Chloe!"

Chloe pulled back, hissing, confused.

Brittany tossed the towel toward her and the heavy folds settled over the gray cat.

"Aaaah!" The towel muffled Chloe's cry. She wrestled with it briefly then darted away.

Well done, Jasper thought. He blinked at Brittany with satisfaction and love. *That's my girl.*

She leaned into the bushes toward him again. She lifted him and cradled him close, hands and body warm against his damp sides.

"I'm sorry honey. I know the bath was awful and I don't know why Chloe's being so mean to you. Maybe she's jealous."

Jasper hummed against her.

She gazed at him with half-closed eyes, stroking his head, murmuring to him.

"You're a special cat, aren't you? You're my boy. I know you're magic. You understand me, don't you, Lucky?"

Jasper purred deep in his chest and looked straight back at her. *This is why they're so important to me. Nothing else in the world comes close to this feeling.*

"Goodness!" Hank said from a nearby tree. He lifted his wings and shook them, quivered all over.

Yes, that's exactly it. Jasper closed his eyes. It was curious the way they seemed to need something mute and close to the earth to love. That was the real magic. Humans were inexplicable: tall and loud and sometimes cruel, but when they opened up and turned that love on you, it was like a fierce, intoxicating light searching for something they had lost.

Of course it had just been the children who'd given it to him. Was it like the big-headed awkwardness of kittens, something they outgrew? Then he remembered the frosty-haired woman. She hadn't turned it on him full force, like the focused flame of the brown-eyed boy and Brittany, but he could feel the low-level hum, the steady warmth of her affection. He suspected that Precious got the full effect.

Brittany carried him to a place in the sun and spread the towel on the grass. He lay on her stomach, head pushed into her hands, nudging them whenever the scratching and stroking slowed. Her belly had that warm springy softness that made him think of his mother and he began to knead her chest ever so gently.

"It's going to be so nice to have you inside," she said. "I wish I could take you to school with me. I have to start again soon."

Jasper hummed and kneaded and forgave her entirely for the bath.

"I wish I could take you with me," she said softly.

School, he thought. *The boy had gone to school.* The school business had taken the boy away for long stretches of time. He stiffened a little.

"Jasper," Hank said from the pine tree closest to where they lay in the grass.

"Mmm?" Jasper didn't open his eyes, hoped Hank would see that he was busy and leave him alone.

"Jasper, we've got to go." There was an urgent undertone in his voice.

"Listen to that owl," Brittany said and sat up straight, sliding Jasper down into a heap in her lap. "Isn't that your friend, Lucky?"

"It's Chloe," Hank said. "She's gone down the block where the Doberman lives."

Fine, Jasper thought. *Let her go. I was just getting comfortable.*

Hank spread his wings and with a soft throaty rush of air, took off.

"Where's he going?" Brittany stood and shaded her eyes, trying to track Hank.

Jasper sat for a moment, composing himself. He stood and stretched his limbs and felt that he was mostly dry. Slowly, he began to walk in the direction that Hank had gone.

"Where are you going, Lucky? Wait for me!" She scrambled to put the floppy shoes on her feet.

He thought of the intent angular face of the dog, jaws slightly open, big feet padding softly, with such purpose. *Not a good idea for her to come along.* He started to run, a quick burst of speed to leave her behind.

Chapter 11

HE SUN WAS STILL BRILLIANT, but, muscular shadowy clouds, like burly unshaven men, had started to gather on one side of the sky. Jasper lifted his head and tasted the air deeply for rain. Maybe later, certainly before dark, it would come. He loved the sweetness of rain in the heat. Mostly gentle, usually cool and soothing, it was as if the broad, mutable face of the sky was offering a gift, a little something to make up for the impassive stare of the sun.

The sun never faltered, Jasper was convinced. It was the sky who kept her in check. The generous sky, who stood with outstretched arms above them, holding them all, the moon, the sun, him and the neighborhood, in a broad, loving hug. The moon had never said so, but that was the way he saw it when things were going well. When things weren't going well, the sky was a remote witness, just watching, like some humans who weren't actively hostile but would let him starve without a second thought.

It didn't take long to get to the big angry man's house, which was on the way to the Doberman's street. He looked around for Max.

No sign of him or the big man. Jasper kept going.

He saw Chloe before she saw him. She was crouched down, tail tip in a low slow wave, eyes fixed on a blue-black butterfly alight on the grass. The butterfly pumped his wings deliberately, hypnotically, and Jasper could feel his own muscles tensing.

The butterfly took flight and Chloe leaped, surprisingly high for a cat of her bulk, and almost nabbed it with one stabbing claw. She landed lightly, staying crouched until she caught sight of him.

Fur bristling, ears back, she hissed. "Get out of here."

"Chloe," he said. "You need to go somewhere else."

She bared her fangs. "You go somewhere else."

"But you don't understand—" He tried to tell her but she cut him off.

"I understand all right." Her tail whipped and she growled. "You're a mangy, wicked stray who wants to push me out of the only home I've every had."

She lunged for him. He ducked and ran, hoping she'd chase him.

"This is my place!" she screamed. "Not yours! I was here first!"

He galloped under the holly bush and brushed too close on one side, feeling the sharp leaf edges.

"Chloe?" Hank said, a disembodied voice from someplace close above them.

Chloe shot into the bushes near Jasper and flattened against the ground. Her breathing was short and labored. She seemed to have forgotten him for the moment in her concern over the owl's whereabouts.

"Chloe," Hank repeated. "There's something you need to know."

She bared her teeth again. "I'll tear your eyes out, I swear."

"We're not here to hurt you," Hank said. "But there's a dog that's going to try and attack you. A Doberman."

"Dog, schmog," Chloe growled, low and continuous. "There's something twisted about the two of you. It's not right for a cat to be friends with an owl. Why don't you just leave me alone?" She ended with a shriek and took off across the yard like she'd been stung by a bee.

The two of them sat without speaking, listening to the echo of her cry drift away in the yawn of the wind. The wind was growing more restless, beginning to stretch and push among the trees. Jasper glanced up at the sky. More clouds, more shadows.

"That went well," he said.

"You think so?" Hank blinked down from his branch.

Jasper shook his head. "No, Hank, I'm making a joke. She hates me and she's scared to death of you. She didn't believe a word we said."

Hank clicked his beak. "That's exactly what I thought."

They sat in silence again. The faint rattle of dog tags made them both straighten and look toward the street.

Jasper peered out through the branches of the holly. "Can you see who that is?"

Hank stared down the street. "It's the Doberman. And it looks like Max is with him."

That's good, Jasper thought. *Max is on top of it.*

They both watched as the Doberman swung his head and caught sight of something that made him freeze. They couldn't see Chloe from where they were, but Jasper had a sick feeling about what the sudden point of interest was.

The bigger dog started across the grass toward the back yard, ears pointed forward, his gait springy but controlled. Max started right after him, bit playfully at his neck. The Doberman shrugged him off once, twice, then growled deep in his chest. Max stood square and barked at him. The big dog leaped into a hard run and Max quickly fell behind.

"Time to move." Hank stretched his wings and took flight.

Jasper stepped out of the bushes, and keeping a careful eye on various escape routes up the trees, trotted across the front yard. He got to the side of the house and noticed there was a long stretch without any trees. He also noticed Chloe in a corner of the back yard, stalking a small bird perched on a low limb of a crape myrtle tree. Head down, belly hugging the ground like a small gray panther, Chloe was transfixed. *A small deaf panther*, he thought. *How did she miss the commotion in the front yard?*

The Doberman had slowed to a bouncy trot. He came closer. He tensed for the final dash. A gray-brown blur swooped from above. To Jasper's horror, Hank flew right at the Doberman's head. The dog ducked and kept coming. Chloe finally looked up. She saw the monstrous dog, three leaps away and she froze.

Jasper couldn't stand it. He ran toward the dog, yowling as loudly as he could. Max came barking, loping around the house and they nearly collided. They both ran for the Doberman, who stopped and lifted his head toward the two of them, the yowling cat and barking dog galloping straight at him.

"Run, Chloe, run!" Jasper screamed. Finally, she seemed to wake up. She sprang away.

Jasper and Max didn't slow down. Hank dove again and this time, the Doberman lunged for him. Jasper was a step ahead of Max. He sprang and landed on the dog's head, legs stretched long, claws slashing. The Doberman yelped. Max crashed into his side and the big dog fell. Jasper leaped and hit the ground running as hard as he ever had.

There was a terrible growling and snarling and thumping behind him. Shrieks of pain. He stopped and leaped up a small tree to look back.

Max was on his back. The Doberman stood over him.

"So what was that all about, you idiot?" The big dog's snarling face was close to Max's throat. "What kind of dog are you?"

"I was going for the ugly one, Brutus." Max's voice was breathless. "I was chasing him and I just got all caught up. You know how it is."

"You didn't look like you were chasing him. You ran right into me, you moron. Why'd you do that?"

Max squirmed. "Like I said, I was going for him."

"Clumsy mutt," the bigger dog shook his head and stepped away. Jasper was gratified to see a set of long red scratches on one side of his face. "Craziest thing I ever saw." The Doberman lifted his head and looked around. "And what was that bird doing?"

Max stood up, shook himself. "What bird?"

"Didn't you see that crazy bird, diving at my head like an overgrown horsefly?"

Max cocked his head. "A bird? Are you sure?"

The Doberman stiffened. "Of course I'm sure. What do you think, I would make up something like that?" He sat down. "It was a big bird. Like some kind of hawk or maybe a crow."

A series of indignant hoots came from a nearby tree. Jasper smiled to himself.

Max shrugged. "I don't know. First you think that me and some cat are coming at you. Now you're saying this crow was in on it too?"

The Doberman jumped up. "Forget it. Let's go to the creek."

The two dogs trotted off.

"Crow?" Hank said. "Is there anything about me that looks like a crow?"

Jasper smiled. *Mr. Goody Do-Right has a weakness.*

"Weakness?" Hank twisted his head. "What's weak? If that silly dog can't tell an owl from a crow, I'd say the weakness is his eyesight."

"You are so right, Hank." Jasper started to walk back to Brittany's. "Did you see where Chloe went?"

"Probably back home."

He walked and Hank flew and it wasn't long before they were in Brittany's back yard again. Chloe lay on the deck, tail hanging down like a fat fishing line.

"Hi, Chloe." Jasper trotted up to the deck and looked up at her.

Hank lighted on the smooth arm of an old oak.

She sniffed and turned her face away. Jasper hopped up to the deck.

"Hello, Chloe." He sat down directly in front of her.

"Hello," she said, still not looking at him.

"I see you got home all right," Jasper persisted.

She blinked at him and her tail twitched a little. "Of course."

He waited. She closed her eyes.

"Thought we were going to have some real trouble back there, didn't you?" He tried one more time.

"Trouble?" She pulled herself up to sit on her haunches and licked one paw. Began scrubbing her face.

"Yes, trouble." He leaned in closer to her. "Why can't you just say it?"

"Jasper," Hank said. Jasper ignored him.

She stared at the cat like he was a young, bothersome human. "Say what?"

"Thank you!" He stood up. "You might say, 'Thank you,' to me and Hank and, 'Gee, you were right. I was wrong to misjudge you and I really appreciate you two saving my life!'"

The plump gray cat continued bathing herself. She stopped and licked her lips thoughtfully. She jumped down to the ground and walked away, tail flagged straight up in the air.

Jasper watched her, his tail thumping the deck. "What is the matter with her? Doesn't she know how to say thank you? Doesn't she appreciate what we did for her?"

"She just doesn't know how to say it," Hank said.

"Easy. Two words. Thank you."

"It may seem easy to you, but for Chloe…" Hank shook his big head.

"He's right." The voice from under the deck startled both of them. Joey stepped out from the shadows underneath the platform and hopped up beside Jasper. "She told me what you two did. And she wasn't sure, but she said maybe the big angry man's dog helped. How did you manage that?"

Jasper swelled up a little. "Oh, he's not a bad dog when you get to know him."

Hank clicked his beak.

"They're all bad dogs as far as I'm concerned," Joey shuddered. "Never met one yet that didn't want to tear me apart."

Jasper stretched out in the sun and closed his eyes.

"So why'd you do it?" Joey said.

Jasper shrugged. "I'm beginning to ask myself the same question."

"Oh stop it, Jasper," Hank shook his wings. "You shouldn't say that. You don't do what you do to make others be nice to you."

"I don't?" Jasper didn't open his eyes.

"Then why?" Joey said, sitting down in front of Jasper.

Jasper twitched his ear.

"Because it needed doing," Hank said. "It's as simple as that. We knew Chloe was going to be in trouble and something needed to be done so we did it."

"But you don't like her," Joey stared at Jasper. "And she hates you."

"Doesn't make sense, does it?" Jasper said. He opened his eyes without lifting his head. "I don't understand it." He glanced toward Hank. "Ask him. He's the one with all the answers."

Joey turned his head to look at the owl, who blinked his big yellow eyes.

The door to the deck opened. Nathan stood in the doorway.

"Kitties!" He shouted with joy. He took a few fast, flat-footed steps. Joey melted away over the edge of the deck. Jasper raised his head and watched the boy.

He squatted by the cat and slowly raised his hand to Jasper's face. Jasper sniffed politely and caught the smell of the boy, like popcorn and Play-doh and a hint of the grape bubble gum he associated with Brittany.

"Nice kitty." Nathan's hand was a little too heavy on his back and his head, but something in the boy's dark eyes made him stay. He watched as the boy knelt down and touched his cheek to Jasper's. "Good kitty."

Jasper blinked. Memories of the brown-eyed boy washed over him. This boy had eyes of dark green flecked with gold and he moved like a jerky young child but there was something of the first boy's sweetness. He licked the boy's cheek.

The boy grew still then licked Jasper's head. Astonished, Jasper stared at him.

"Nathan!" Brittany's mother stood in the doorway. "What are you doing? You know better than that. You don't lick the kitty." She stepped behind the boy, grasped him under the arms and stood him up. The boy's face crumpled.

Jasper slipped over the edge of the deck and crept underneath to lie near Joey.

"Hey, it's not bad under here," he said. "Nice and cool."

"That's why I like it," Joey said. "Chloe always says it's too dirty or muddy or something but I like it."

"Kitty!" the boy shouted from the deck.

"Lucky." Brittany stood in the yard. "His name is Lucky."

"Wucky!" Nathan smiled at his big sister.

"He's fallen in love with that cat," the woman said to Brittany.

"I know." Brittany squatted to see under the deck. "Lucky?"

Jasper left the dark comfort below the deck to twist around her legs. Brittany picked him up and put him on the deck. She scratched his head and Nathan patted his back with a careful flat hand.

"He kissed me," Nathan said to Brittany.

"Really?"

"Right here." He poked his cheek.

"Let's go inside and have lunch." The woman opened the door and waved her hand.

Brittany picked Jasper up again. "I gave him a bath this morning, Mom. I'm going to bring him inside."

The woman squinted at Jasper, her mouth a worried, working

line. He was sprawled in Brittany's arms, while Nathan, who could only reach the cat's stomach, kept rubbing it, leaning against Brittany like she was a friendly wall.

Please, Mom, Jasper thought.

The woman leaned close and pretended she smelled the air. "Well, I suppose." She smoothed Brittany's hair and gripped Nathan's shoulder. "He certainly is good-natured, isn't he? I don't remember Chloe or Joey letting Nathan touch them."

"They don't," Brittany said as she walked to the door. "They're good cats but they're nothing like Lucky."

"Wucky!" Nathan said, as he struggled to move with Brittany and keep his hand on some small part of Jasper.

Lucky indeed, Jasper thought, as the door closed behind them.

Chapter 12

HE DOOR TO THE DECK OPENED into a big room with a low tight carpet the color of old snow. With each step, Jasper felt his claws sink into the softness and he had to work each foot free, lifting it high.

"Look at the kitty," Nathan pointed at Jasper and laughed.

Brittany giggled. "He looks like he's walking through something sticky."

Jasper slunk down at the sound of their laughter and they shrieked louder. He went to the edges of the room, behind the chairs and the television table. He took fast fluttery sniffs of the cool, settled air, away from the glare of the late summer sun. Inside air didn't have that heavy, rich feel to it of the outside; inside it was thin, layered with human smells and the strong, strange odors that went with them.

Another smell hung in the air, behind all the others like a welcoming wall: the smell of food. It was the smell of comfort and sweet security, of knowing that something tasty was available any time at all inside this collection of smooth-walled boxes. The food smells had sifted and settled into the fibers of the rug; complex, subtle, and lovely. Jasper quivered with the perfect promise of it.

"He's cold!" Nathan pointed at him.

"He's not cold." Brittany knelt beside him as he sniffed around the fireplace. "He's excited. He's not used to being inside."

He brushed against her and hurried on. *So much to smell, so much to take in.*

"How about showing him where the litter box is." The woman watched Jasper, hands on her hips. "Surely he'll know how to use it."

"Okay." Brittany picked Jasper up and took him down a short hallway to a small compact bathroom with a shower, commode, and sink. Between the commode and the shower, pushed up against the wall, was a small litter box.

Jasper was struck by the commode. Porcelain white and smooth, it reminded him of birdbaths that he had seen in back yards in the neighborhood. He thought he smelled water. He braced his paws against the side and stretched his neck to look inside. Water, sure enough. Brittany reached over him and flushed.

He ran at the sudden loud sound. When the noise chortled away as Brittany laughed, he stepped back around the doorframe, hugging the wall, ready to run again.

"Look, Lucky," Brittany gripped a corner of the litter box and shook it. "You know what this is for."

Jasper considered the pristine gray invitation of the box. He stepped in and sniffed. No sign of any other cats. He looked at Brittany and hoped she'd take the hint and give him some private time.

Sure enough, she turned and walked out. He finished his business, scratched about the box then stepped out. The box was his and his alone.

A feeling of inexplicable joy seized his heart and bounced it hard. He ran from the bathroom with abandon. Down the hallway, into the family room, through Nathan's ankles and around the legs of the woman. They laughed as he dashed around the room and truly, gloriously, for once, Jasper didn't care.

The kitchen was a bright, warm affair with a hard smooth floor. *Hard to get any traction. One extreme to the next,* Jasper thought. He lay in the middle of the floor, between the table and the refrigerator. The tall woman pulled plates from a cabinet near the sink. Nathan and Brittany sat at the table, the boy's hand stretched flat over a sheet of paper while she traced the outline with a pencil.

"Now see?" She sat back and moved his hand. "Here's a fresh sheet, you do the other one."

Nathan spread his other hand on the clean paper. Slowly, his mouth open, he worked the pencil through his fingers.

"Good!" Brittany said. "That's really good, Nathan."

The woman stood at the refrigerator. "What do you guys want—turkey or ham?"

"Turkey," Brittany said. Nathan nodded vigorously.

She opened the door and Jasper stepped close and pushed his head in to see. He had imagined possible rooms full of food, but a box, a shiny cold box filled with all sorts of faint mysterious food smells, was a dream he hadn't considered. *There's meat in there, I'm sure of it.*

"Well, look at Mr. Helpful." The woman spoke to him. "Do you want to make the sandwiches, Lucky?"

He looked up at her, squeezing his eyes into submissive eye kisses.

"You little flirt." She bent down and rubbed his head.

He blinked at her. The only thing about the refrigerator business was that it was darned cold. Nevertheless, he poked his head in as far as he could reach while she pulled bags and jars from the box and pulled away only when she closed the door with her foot.

He sat, polite and attentive, while she washed her hands and made the sandwiches. It was real meat she was working with; he could smell it. She glanced at him as she held the bag of sliced turkey then looked over at Brittany and Nathan who were engrossed in drawing something. She tore off a sliver of turkey and tossed it toward him. He snatched it out of the air. *Ahhhhhhh.*

The woman smiled and pulled a bag of chips from the cabinet. She loaded each plate with a handful or two and carried them to the table. He hurried behind, struggling to swallow the turkey and rub against her legs in adoration and hopes for more. The woman sat down with the children and they all ate while Jasper stretched out on the cool floor.

"So Brittany, are you ever going to tell me why you think he's magic?" The woman looked at Jasper.

Brittany shook her head. "You wouldn't believe me."

The woman shrugged. "I might not. That doesn't mean you would have to stop believing it."

She gave her mother an assessing look. "You can't tell Rick."

"Why not?"

Brittany took a big bite of her sandwich and chewed deliberately. "He'd make fun of me."

"Rick wouldn't make fun of you, honey. I really wish you'd call him Dad." The woman scanned their plates. "Eat your sandwich, Nathan."

Brittany squirmed in her seat. "He's not my dad," she mumbled under her breath. "My dad lives in Seattle. And he already made fun of Lucky. So I wouldn't want him to know."

The woman sighed. They ate in silence until Nathan began to hum. Brittany chewed on a tortilla chip and studied the half-eaten chip with a sudden great interest.

"He knows things. He helps people, and probably other animals." She crossed her arms over her chest. "And he's friends with this owl."

"Ow, ow, ow," Nathan bounced in his seat and laughed. Chip fragments rattled on the floor and Jasper hurried over, smooth as a shadow, to examine the food. He crunched a piece. *Salty, hard, brittle. Not bad, but nothing like the turkey.*

"Did he help you?" The woman reached over the table and tapped Nathan's plate. "If you don't finish your sandwich, there'll be no PlayStation this afternoon." She turned her attention back to Brittany. "What did he do?"

Brittany glanced at Jasper. "First, he helped Nathan one day in the woods. Somebody was picking on him and Lucky tripped him. It was pretty funny." She smiled to herself. "Then, another time, these boys were trying to scare me and Lucky came and kept me company and the big owl scared the boys instead."

Jasper groomed his back leg and smiled to himself with the memory of that evening in the graveyard.

"What boys?" The woman straightened in her chair. "Who picked on Nathan and tried to scare you, Brittany? Was it that Bennington boy?"

Brittany sighed and shrugged.

"You know I don't like you playing with that boy."

"We weren't playing." Brittany picked up her plate and walked to the sink. Jasper jumped up and followed her, trying to see if she had left anything. She rinsed her dish and left it in the sink.

"Nathan, I'm not kidding. Either you finish your sandwich or you go from here to your bedroom for a nap. Brittany, please put your plate in the dishwasher."

Nathan began a continuous, low-pitched hum of protest and stood up.

The woman stood and pointed at his plate. "Finished?"

He turned and ran upstairs. The woman picked up the plates and brought them to the sink. Brittany started to follow the boy upstairs. Jasper stretched and rose to his feet.

"Brittany."

The girl stopped in the doorway.

"I need for you to wipe off the table." The woman rinsed the plates.

Brittany pulled a paper towel from the roll and waved it under the water running in the sink.

"I thought I told you how I felt about Tyler Bennington." The woman slid the dishes into the dishwasher and closed the chip bag with much crackling and rustling.

Brittany wiped the table with long arcs and said nothing. Jasper sat and began to groom that part of his chest that he could reach.

"Did you hear what I said?" The woman pushed her hair back from her face and put one fist on her hip.

"Yes, ma'am," Brittany said. She stood in front of her mother, looking pointedly at the cabinet door where the trashcan was kept.

"So you understand that I don't want you doing things with him." The woman stood firmly positioned in front of the cabinet.

Brittany lifted her eyes to her mother's face. "Why don't you like him?"

"It's not that I don't like him." The woman reached out and smoothed Brittany's hair. "I'm sure he's really a nice boy. It's just he's older than you and he's done some things that your father and I don't approve of."

"What did he do?" Brittany's eyes were steady on her mother's.

"Well," the woman hesitated.

"He's not mean to Nathan anymore," said Brittany.

The woman's mouth opened and closed.

Brittany looked at the floor. "He didn't mean anything by it. He said he was sorry." She lifted her head and met the woman's eyes again. "You know, sometimes Cole isn't very nice to Nathan either."

The woman hugged Brittany, stiff and unresponsive, to her chest. "Oh, sweetie."

After a few seconds, Brittany began to push away. "It's okay, Mom." She reached behind the woman and threw her wadded paper towel away.

The girl bounded up the stairs, Jasper a step or two behind. She led the way into a room with a small bed covered with a dark blue comforter. A poster of a baseball player deep in the curl of a homerun swing was pinned over the bed. Another wall was covered with a quarterback, his arm cocked, his face fierce with concentration in the search for that elusive free receiver. Nathan lay on his bed, hugging a Nerf football and singing softly, tunelessly along with the sound that blared from a radio.

Jasper jumped on the bed. Nathan squealed with delight. He reached too quickly and the cat shrunk away.

"Easy." Brittany sat on the bed and Jasper crawled to her lap. "You have to move slow or you scare him."

Nathan scooted toward her and stretched his arm so slowly his hand quivered. He touched Jasper's fur and stroked the curve of his back.

"Good kitty," he breathed.

Lucky kitty, Jasper thought, safe in the bony pocket of Brittany's lap. *She won't get bored with me. I won't allow it. And how could I make any mistakes? I'm the magic cat.*

He smiled a secret cat smile to himself and wondered idly what Hank might be doing. Probably dozing in a shady glen somewhere, waiting for the night and the stark pale face of the moon. A small shiver rippled through the cat as he closed his eyes and sank into the velvet womb of sleep.

Chapter 13

INSIDE THE HOUSE was an intoxicating new world for Jasper. At first, he kept his exploring to a minimum, but after a few weeks, he felt bored and restless.

One afternoon while Brittany and Nathan sat on the blue bed, coloring and reading, Jasper rambled about the upstairs. He padded into the room with a wide bed cornered with carved wooden poles on a smooth rug alive with intricate designs. The air smelled of faint flowers and musk; Jasper guessed it was where the tall woman and the man slept. Jasper found a flashing gold hoop earring on top of the dresser and swatted it to the floor for a chase but it got stuck in the rug and wouldn't move well after that.

He walked down the hall and found Brittany's room. The orange and green bedspread was tossed over rumpled sheets and the floor was still covered with stuffed animals, books, and balls. Jasper reached out and tapped a barrette, interested in the way it skittered and spun on the floor. He chased it across the floor until he swatted it under the white table with the filmy skirt.

He brushed against the gauzy material, tantalized by the feel of it. He pawed at it, stretched out his claws and hooked it. The table rattled as he pulled his claw free and the fabric tore easily. He rolled on his back to wrestle with the tatters. The fabric amused him for a few minutes then he stepped back to survey the top. With one smooth jump, he was up beside the shoes.

The tiny soft shoes had ribbons instead of laces and Jasper couldn't resist the urge to swat one and watch the ribbons stream behind it as it flew off the table. He jumped after the slipper and slipped on the smooth top of the table. Scrambling, he slid into the lamp and he, the lamp, and the tiny ivory cat fell from the table. The chink of something breaking came from close by and Jasper shot under the bed.

"Lucky!" Brittany screamed as she ran into the room and it wasn't a happy scream. Jasper recognized the tone; he'd heard it when he'd ripped into a woman's garbage and was picking through the remnants for tasty bits to eat. He tensed and crawled to the farthest corner of the bed, away from the scream.

"Lucky!" Brittany sounded like she was crying. "Look what you did!"

Jasper crouched down, his mouth dry, heart beating hard. *What did I do? I was just playing.*

"What?" Nathan thumped into the room and spoke in his curious jumbled way. "What happened, Bree?"

"He broke it! And he tore the table!" Brittany knelt down and picked up one of the slippers that had fallen to the floor with Jasper and the lamp. She sniffed and walked on her knees over to the lamp. She picked it up and ran her fingers over the broken arm and nose of the ballerina built into the base. She touched the gauzy fabric that Jasper had shredded and cupped the ivory cat to her chest.

"Oh, Lucky." Her head and shoulders drooped and she shook her head as she sobbed. Nathan crept up behind her and touched her head. She sobbed louder. Footsteps sounded up the stairs and stopped outside the door.

"Brittany?" The tall woman crossed the room with a few long strides and bent to study Brittany, then Nathan's face. "Are you all

right? Nathan, are you hurt?"

"He broke it," Brittany said. "He ripped Alicia's table. He ruined it." She held up the lamp. "He knocked her lamp off the table and broke it."

"Nathan?" The tall woman gave Nathan a stern, resigned look.

"No, no. Lucky." Brittany buried her face in her hands.

"Oh, sweetie." The tall woman knelt beside Brittany and gathered her in a hug. Brittany pressed against her mother and cried softly. Nathan patted her head.

The tall woman looked over Brittany's head at the table skirt that Jasper had shredded. "I think I can fix it."

"It can't be fixed." Brittany said and pulled away. She sat for a moment and stared at the table. "Why did he do it?"

"I'm sure he didn't mean any harm," the tall woman said. "He was just doing what kitties do."

"But I told you, Lucky's not a regular cat." Brittany shook her head and stood up. She looked around the room. "Where is he? Lucky?"

Under the bed, Jasper tried to shrink and licked his dry mouth.

"Brittany," the tall woman said. "It's not his fault."

"It is!" Brittany said. She went to the closet and swiveled her head to scan the inside. "He should know better."

"Honey, he's just a cat." The tall woman touched the girl on the shoulder.

"No!" Brittany jerked away from the touch. "He's not! He's smarter than that. He should know about Alicia."

The tall woman sighed and sat on the bed.

Brittany shook her head and knelt beside the bed. She lifted the bedspread up so she could look underneath. "There you are. Bad boy! Bad Lucky!"

Jasper shot out from under the bed, then out the door and down the stairs. No place to hide in the kitchen. He rounded the corner and ran back to the family room. The couch was too low to crawl under so he wedged himself between a big leather chair and the wall. He peered at the glass door. Was it wishful thinking or did he hear footsteps thumping on the deck? The thudding sounded closer. When the door slid open, he was coiled and ready. He bounded across the room keeping his claws pulled in tight. Brittany's brother Cole stepped inside when Jasper slipped by him like a soft mottled shadow.

The air outside was thick and hot and alive with scent after the diluted cool of the inside. Jasper took quick, fluttery breaths to get his bearings. He loped out to the grass and rolled with pleasure. The dry grass felt like a friendly feathery brush against his back and sides and the top of his head. *How nice it feels to be outside again.* He rested on his back, feet in the air and dozed in the companionable gaze of the afternoon sun.

"Jasper?" Hank's voice sounded close.

"Hello, Hank," he said.

"What happened?"

Jasper stared at the pale sky and tried to make his mind as blank as the broad blue expanse. "It was lovely. Perfection. All I ever dreamed of."

"Something happened. Why is Brittany so upset?" Hank wouldn't let it alone.

Jasper rolled to his side and lolled in the grass, flicking his tail. "Something about this stuff I was playing with. There's this lamp that got broken."

"What did you do?"

Jasper sat up and saw Hank's yellow eyes in the thick leaves of the willow tree. "I was just playing a little with this stuff in Brittany's room. I've never seen anything like it, Hank. It was like a cloud but you could touch it and it tore in these wispy little pieces, just like a cloud would." He sighed.

"And the lamp?" Hank blinked.

"It was an accident. I was playing with these shoes, these soft shoes with ribbons, and the top of the table was just too smooth. They shouldn't make things that smooth. How are you supposed to get any traction?" Jasper twisted around to groom his back.

Hank was quiet for a few long minutes while the crickets began to creak in the shadow of the afternoon sun. "So there are things inside you're not supposed to touch?"

"Just a few." Jasper worked harder on his back, trying to reach the top of his tail.

"Places you're not supposed to go?"

"I suppose." Jasper stood and stretched. "Have you seen Chloe and Joey lately?"

"They're around front." Hank lifted his wings and settled himself on the branch.

"I need a nap." Jasper walked to the bushes and found a comfortable coolish place in the dappled light. He reclined, closed his eyes, and dozed.

The sliding glass door rumbled open.

"Lucky!" Brittany said as she stood on the deck.

Jasper stayed where he was, listening carefully for any hint of anger in her tone.

"Lucky? Where are you, boy?" She called again and still Jasper didn't move.

"I'm sorry I yelled at you. You're not a bad boy. Lucky?" Her voice was definitely not angry any more. Jasper walked slowly out of the bushes, stopping to stretch by walking his front paws forward, letting his back end drop in a long, luxurious stretch.

"Lucky!" Brittany hurried off the deck toward him. He rubbed around her calves and she squatted down to gather him in a hug.

"You just can't touch Alicia's table." She hugged him hard until he squeaked. She let him go, but cradled his head in her hands and brought her face close to his.

"Alicia was my twin sister. She got hit by a car and died." She kept looking at him with her big light eyes like she was searching for something. He looked back at her, wondering if there was something to see in those round black centers.

"You need to leave her things alone." Brittany said. "Do you understand?"

Jasper squirmed. *No, I don't. Not really.*

She released him finally and turned back toward the house. "Well, come on then. Let's go back inside."

He sat for a moment in the lovely coarse grass, dried out from the summer sun. He looked around at the generous, patient trees, up at the unreadable sky. Then the thought of all the food inside the cold shiny box came back to him. He trotted to catch up with her.

After dinner, Brittany read a book and Nathan colored with Jasper curled between them while the infernal radio box blazed. Jasper dozed in and out, mostly out for long stretches when his mind hummed into one smooth lovely expanse, creamy and complete as a bowl of milk. He'd heard talk of a better thing called cream, heavy as blood and rich with flavor, but he'd never had the pleasure of tasting it. So the thought of milk would have to do.

Nathan mumbled and reached over Jasper to shake Brittany's arm.

"That's good." Brittany looked at the vivid scribbling on the page he held out. "I like the purple." She leaned closer to the picture. "You gave him purple hair, Nathan."

"And green." He spoke so quickly his words ran together.

"Purple and green hair. That's very nice." She smiled at him and the boy glowed and settled back.

Jasper dozed, breathing the warm house air until the soft thud of footsteps stopped outside the door, and the pungent smell of a teenage boy drifted into range. The young man anchored one hand on each side of the doorway and leaned into the room. Jasper tensed, ready to hop to the floor and take cover as he remembered the times he had been chased by boys Cole's age. The size and heaviness of Cole's feet concerned him even though he had ignored the cat thus far.

Brittany glanced at him. "Hey, Cole."

"Hey princess. You two making great art?"

Nathan nodded vigorously and held his picture out to Cole.

"Oh yeah." Cole bent over and squinted at the drawing. "You

captured it all right. I'm not sure exactly what you captured but you definitely got something."

Nathan looked back at the picture with interest.

"I got it." Cole held up a finger. "It's measles. That's what you've got. All over you." He poked Nathan's shirt in a few spots, and when the younger boy looked down, chucked him under the chin.

Nathan looked baffled until Cole laughed. Then Nathan smiled too and poked Brittany and Jasper with soft, experimental jabs. Jasper jumped to the floor and sat down a safe distance away.

"Measles!" Nathan said.

After the poking and giggling subsided, Cole sat down beside Brittany.

"Gotta question for you, Miss B." He leaned back on his elbows.

"No, you can't use my new soccer ball." She opened her book and settled back against the wall.

"Not what I was going to say." He flicked lightly at her hair.

"You can't have my bottle rockets." She kept her head down, eyes fixed on the page in front of her.

"You still have bottle rockets? Cool." Cole sat up and tapped her leg. "Mom might be interested in knowing that."

Brittany kept her eyes on the open book.

"Strike two." He shook his head. "Two out. Bottom of the ninth. Two men on base. A sacrifice fly won't get it, ladies and gentlemen. What we need is a clean base hit." He looked at Brittany expectantly.

"Strike two!" Nathan could no longer contain himself and still sitting, bounced on the bed.

"No," said Brittany. "Whatever it is, no."

"Aw, come on, B." Cole leaned back on his elbows, let his head drop back. "And to think I was actually considering helping you."

"Helping me?" She lifted her face toward him. "Helping me do what?"

Cole nodded in Jasper's direction. "Heard that Mr. Lucky had himself a little party in your bedroom. Broke your lamp and all."

Brittany narrowed her eyes. "Who told you that? It was no big deal."

Cole shrugged. "What difference does it make? Anyway, I thought maybe I could give you a hand gluing your lamp back together, that's all."

She studied Cole for a long moment. "No, thanks anyway."

"No? What are you going to do, leave it broken?"

She shrugged. "Maybe."

"Suit yourself." Cole stood up.

"What was it you wanted?" She looked up at him.

"Ah, forget it." He waved a hand and walked to the door. "I was just wondering if you're planning to go visit your dad this summer. You and Nathan, you know, like you usually do. I've got a couple of buddies from Asheville I met on the state team and I was thinking if you didn't mind, they could come for a visit. Use your rooms while you're out of town."

Nathan had his head down, mouth working as he labored over a new picture. He looked up at the sound of his name.

"Dad?" he said.

Brittany grimaced and looked down at the book. "I don't think so."

Nathan bent down and twisted his head to look up into her face. "Bree? We go see Dad?"

She shook her head. "I don't know, Nathan. He just changed jobs and he said it might not be the best time. Maybe Christmastime." She thought for a minute. "I don't think I'd want anybody I didn't know in my room anyway."

"Okay." Cole turned to leave.

"Cole?" Brittany said. He stopped.

"Maybe Nathan could stay in my room and they could share his," she said slowly. "We could ask Mom."

Nathan sat and bounced again.

"That would be stellar." Cole nodded. "Thanks."

Chapter 14

HE NIGHTS WERE UNBEARABLY LONG to Jasper. Curled beside Brittany while she read in the bright hard funnel of light over her bed, he tried to relax. She reached out every so often to stroke his side or his head but when she rested her hand on him, it became heavy and hot. He had to nudge her fingers or stand up to reposition. She fell asleep, the book spread on her chest. Jasper closed his eyes and tried to sleep in the harsh glare of the lamp.

How could the sun work her way inside to shine at night? He wondered. The source of light did seem very small and not nearly so blinding as the larger version in the sky, but it had to be related, Jasper figured. He blinked and closed his eyes, pretending the heat from the light was his own miniature sun. *Humans could be so clever. Clearly they had found a way to breed the sun and train her little ones in helpful ways.*

The tall woman came in the room and gently plucked the book from the sleeping girl. Jasper stood up and meowed a short greeting.

"Sweet boy," she said and stroked his head. She looked at

Brittany. In sleep, the girl looked younger than her years, tender as new grass. The tall woman pulled the comforter up around Brittany then stopped and looked at the white table. She looked at it for a long time before she sat on the satin bench and touched the framed photograph. She picked up the ivory cat, rubbed it against her cheek. Then she traced a finger over the broken nose of the ballerina and rubbed the place where her arm had snapped off. Head bowed, she stayed that way for such a long moment Jasper thought she had fallen asleep, too.

Finally, she clicked on the nightlight beside the vanity. When she reached over the bed to turn off the light, Jasper could see that her eyes were shiny, cheeks wet. He meowed again to let her know that he was available if she needed some company.

The woman smiled as if she understood. Her face curved in the shadow of the nightlight.

"Good boy," she said in a soft, low voice. She studied him. "Maybe you're here to let her know it's time to put the table away, huh? You keep knocking things over, there won't be much left. "

He watched her. She pulled the door almost closed as she left.

Jasper sniffed at Brittany, and she murmured and curled on her side into the pillows. He hopped off the bed and sat in the middle of the rug, considering the room.

The nightlight on the wall, close to the white table, cast a humble little spill of light, but it was enough to make the table skirt glow and shadow like snow under the moon. The ballerina in the lamp danced on with her chipped nose and her missing arm, intent to eternity on the music playing just for her that only she could hear.

Something about the table upsets the tall woman but it comforts Brittany. Why is that?

Jasper thought. *I'll ask the moon.* He walked to the window but the curtains were drawn. From the bed to the windowsill was a leap but he thought he could make it. And he almost did. Heavier than he'd ever been from all the regular meals, Jasper made the edge with his front paws, but his hindquarters didn't follow so easily. He tried to hang on but the strain was just too much on his front legs and he had to drop. Second try was successful; he was able to wobble on the edge for a few precious seconds, long enough to see the dark sky and the big oak outside the window. *No view here.*

He left Brittany's room and padded downstairs. The windows in the room beside the front door were set low, starting just above the baseboard, but were covered with heavy drapes. Jasper pushed behind the drapes but the only thing he could see was the leafless backs of the front shrubs, branches stretched wide against each other in their lingering, deliberate jostling for position. The bay window pushed out between the bushes, for a view of the front yard and bluish white glow of the streetlights.

Into the kitchen he walked hopefully, thinking he could see moonlight reflected on the hard, shiny floor. No view from the floor, so he jumped to a chair, then the table to get close to the back window. *There, just behind those trees in the back yard.* He thought he saw the bright wedge of her face rising behind the tree line. He sat on a place mat and waited, knowing that the moon moved on her own special schedule but that eventually she would move. He waited, anxious for the sight of her, the chance to talk.

Can she hear me while I'm inside? The thought jolted him. His heart began to jump a little. And whatever he was watching in the sky wasn't moving at all. He scrambled to leave the table and kicked the mat onto the floor.

Down to the family room he thumped, his breath coming faster. He stopped in front of the door to the deck and cried out in frustration when he realized he still couldn't see the moon.

Hank! He thought hard, wanting the big owl to hear him. *Hank, I need to see the moon and I can't.* No sign of Hank. He searched the darkness but saw only a bold squirrel scramble across the deck. The squirrel stopped and looked at Jasper with manic, empty eyes. Jasper growled. *Where are Chloe and Joey?* The squirrel scampered away. Jasper stared out the glass door, aching for the rich dense air and the dark freckled dome of the sky.

———

Morning came with breakfast, of course, then a nap in a fall of sunlight filtering in through the shrubs in the front room. *It's not so bad in here*, Jasper thought to himself. The previous night seemed ages ago with his warm tight belly and the luxury of the freedom to sprawl wherever he chose without looking over his shoulder for a vicious dog or jealous cat.

Brittany carried a big plastic box into the room. Jasper cast an unconcerned glance. She opened a little door on one end and he thought idly how it looked just about the size to carry a cat or two. She picked him up and crooned to him.

"Hey, Lucky. Want to go for a ride?" She nuzzled his face.

He began to tense. Any time he'd ever heard the word "ride," it had not been a good thing. He tried to twist and push his legs against Brittany's chest, but she was too quick for him. She knelt and pushed him into the little box before he could get any leverage.

"Good boy," she said. "We have to go the vet, just to get your shots and everything. Don't worry, now. Everything will be okay."

His mouth went dry and he could feel himself start to shed. He started to cry, the piteous, insistent plea of the cat who knows he is headed somewhere not of his choosing. *Vet* was not familiar; it wasn't *animal shelter* and that was good but *vet* had a harsh unpleasant sound to it and any place one had to go in a portable plastic cage was suspect.

The ride was short even though he cried so much his throat hurt. Brittany sang to him and poked her fingers through the slits in the box that were far too small to be useful as any kind of escape route. The tall woman carried him in the box, thumping gently with each step, into a small square building. Inside, the smells, of sickness and dogs and rancid sharpness he couldn't identify, were overwhelming. He froze. The woman set him down on a chair between her and Brittany. Crouched in his plastic box, he was grateful for the shelter of it.

There was a huge anxious dog in the same room, snorting and gasping and scratching his toenails on the hard floor. Jasper could only see part of him and he stood so close to the man he had to be leashed, but that was small comfort.

"Let me take a look, please," the big dog said. "Loosen up just a little bit and let me take a look around."

"Keep your distance," said another dog he couldn't see, a small dog from the yapping sound of it. "Don't come any closer."

There were voices, lots of muffled voices, doors opening and closing, and a dog somewhere behind the closed doors who barked occasionally, a bored, aimless kind of bark.

"Let me out," the dog in the back said. "Somebody. Don't forget me. Let me out."

The smell of the place began to make him queasy.

Then he saw something through one side of his box, the smooth, supple movement of a relaxed cat. There was something offbeat about her stride. She hopped up on the counter, where she sat down and Jasper could see that she had lost a back leg.

"First time at a vet?"

Jasper was too tense to answer. He couldn't even see the cat properly. *And what's wrong with her, just walking around this scary room like it's nothing? She's only got three legs. Are they going to take one of mine?*

"It's really not so bad." The tabby licked a paw and scrubbed at her face.

"Do you live here?" Jasper finally managed to speak although his voice sounded strained and unfamiliar. *Why would they cut off her leg? To keep her inside?* His stomach began to knot and twist.

"Sure." The tabby walked down the counter to rub against a short woman talking on the telephone. The short woman stroked the tabby while she spoke.

"—tomorrow morning eight o'clock. See you then." The woman hung up the phone and scratched the tabby's chin. "Is nobody paying any attention to you, Tripod?"

The short woman looked down at a big lined pad, then up toward the tall woman. "Lucky Rogers?"

The tall woman stood and picked up Jasper's box. "That's us. Let's go, Brittany."

They walked into a small room and the tall woman put Jasper's box on a shiny silver shelf that extended from the wall into the middle of the room. He sat in the box and tried to make himself as small as possible. Brittany stood so she faced the side of the box that opened, where the bars were a little wider so she could get almost her whole small hand inside.

"Everything's going to be fine, Lucky." She scratched his chin. "He's really scared."

The tall woman murmured in agreement.

There was a stretch of silence.

"You know, Brittany," the tall woman said. "He may not be the kind of cat that's happy living inside."

Brittany gave no indication that she heard.

"Have you thought about that?" the woman asked.

The girl continued to scratch Jasper, shifting her attention to his ears.

"I know you love him, but you need to think about what's best for him. He might like it a lot better outside with Chloe and Joey."

Brittany shook her head and didn't look at the woman. She began to hum to herself.

The woman sighed.

"You never let me keep anything." Brittany continued to rub Jasper, fiercely, and spoke in a harsh whisper. "You want Lucky to stay outside. You don't like Tyler so I can't be friends with him anymore. You want to throw Alicia's table away."

"Brittany!" the woman said. "How can you say that?"

The door opened and an angular man in a white smock with a long, flexible tube around his neck came into the room.

"Good morning, good morning." He squinted and smiled hard at the tall woman and Brittany. "I'm Dr. Fraser."

"Hello, Dr. Fraser, I'm Laura Ford and this is my daughter Alicia, uh, Brittany Rogers." A mottled dark red crept up the woman's neck toward her face as she extended her hand to the man.

Brittany looked at her mother as if the woman had just vomited on the floor.

"We have two cats that we bring here. Brittany found Lucky roaming around the neighborhood." The woman gestured toward Jasper in the plastic box. "Sweetie, why don't you get him out so Dr. Fraser can take a look at him?"

The man bent over to get a look into the box. He wore big, dark-framed glasses that magnified his eyes and made Jasper think of a praying mantis. "Sure enough, there he is. Hello there, fella."

Brittany swung the door open and peered in. Jasper was crouched down, as close to the opposite end as he could be. The sharp, strange odors of the building hung heavy around the man and his white coat.

Let's get out of here. Jasper looked at Brittany and begged with his eyes. *Please.*

"Come on, Lucky." She gripped him around the middle and pulled him out of the box. The man moved the box to the floor. Jasper stood trembling on the shiny metal table, disliking the slick feel of it under his feet, tensing for the first chance to bolt.

"Thank you, Brittany." The man gripped Jasper and he shrunk away from the strong wiry feel of the hands. "Let's take a look at you." The man stroked his head lightly and Jasper relaxed just a little.

"You're a good-natured fellow aren't you?" The man squeezed him a little and moved his mantis head to look at Jasper closely from all angles. He gently felt the cat's bad back leg. Jasper meowed weakly, a feeble protest.

"So," the man cleared his throat. "He was a stray."

Brittany said nothing, just stared at the man.

"Yes," the tall woman said. "I think he belonged to a little boy whose family moved away a few weeks ago."

The man shook his head and pulled Jasper near him. He put the ends of the scope in his ears, and held the cold disk at the end of the tube against the cat's chest. The man listened for a minute before he pulled the instrument back around his neck.

"We'll take him in the back and get his weight and temperature. Be right back." The man gripped Jasper and opened the door to the inside of the building. The sharp frightening smells intensified. Jasper began to squirm.

The man handed Jasper to a dark woman in a white coat who smelled of coffee and cocoa butter.

"Need his weight and temp please, Beverly." The man walked to another table where two people in white huddled over a small dog.

"Hello there." The woman stroked his head and Jasper relaxed a little. She placed him on a smooth cold metal surface where he crouched tentatively, not wanting to touch anything or lose his balance.

Then it got worse. The woman took a small slim tube, cold as a February morning, and pushed it into his bottom. He yowled in discomfort and dismay.

"It's all right, sweetie. This will just take a minute. Got to get your temperature."

It was all over in a few minutes, and the man carried him back into the room where Brittany and the tall woman waited.

The man lifted Jasper's tail and examined his bottom. He tensed. *Please. Not again.*

"Looks like he's been neutered." He held Jasper's head and lifted his lip to look at his teeth and gums. Jasper twisted and leaned away.

"He hasn't sprayed anything." The tall woman crossed her arms. "We really just wanted to get all his vaccinations up to date. And make sure he was healthy."

"Right." The man straightened up, holding Jasper in place lightly with one hand. "Well, he looks to be pretty fit, except for that back leg."

"What's wrong with his back leg?" Brittany said, her hands back on Jasper.

"Looks like he took a pretty bad hit there, probably a car. Broke the leg, never got set so it healed a little crooked. Probably gets a little stiff, the kind of thing that will bother him more as he gets older."

Jasper trembled and panted as Brittany hugged him. *Is he going to take it off? Please Brittany, don't let him do that.*

"It's a hard life out there for a stray cat. He's very lucky to have found you." The man smiled at Brittany and the tall woman. To Jasper, he looked grim and unreadable; a mantis at work.

"So." The man opened the door to the inside of the building. "I'll get a little help and we'll take care of those shots." He called out to someone in the other room.

"Almost done, boy." Brittany stroked him and with every stroke, he shed another thin layer of hair. Small clumps of his fur dusted the shiny metal surface and scattered on the floor.

Please don't let them take my leg. He burrowed his head into Brittany's chest. *I know it's not perfect but it's really no problem.*

The man came back into the room followed by the dark woman with a small tray. She wore thick gloves.

"Okay, Brittany. I need for you to step back for a minute while we do this," the man said.

"It's better if I hold him," Brittany said.

The man looked at Brittany's mother.

"Brittany, honey, step back and let Dr. Fraser give him the shots," the tall woman said.

"But he's scared." Brittany stayed close to the table, arms wrapped around Jasper.

The tall woman touched Brittany on the shoulder. "Just let them do it. It'll only take a minute then we can take him home and he'll forget all about it."

Sure, Jasper thought. *Forget all about it.*

Brittany slowly stepped away as the technician took firm hold of Jasper's neck and back. The man picked up a syringe from the tray and pulled a handful of loose skin between Jasper's shoulders.

No! Jasper thought. *The orange cat at the shelter. That's what happened to her! Please, no!*

He began to wail, long rolling cries of dread.

The man swabbed his fur with something cold, then jabbed the needle. Jasper flinched and waited. The man rubbed the spot where he'd just stuck the needle.

"Good boy. Just a couple more," the man said.

Several jabs later, a little sore and woozy, Jasper was urged back into the plastic box. He entered without protest and sat in the corner, trying to reach and lick the stinging place where the needles had gone in.

The ride home was short and when Brittany finally opened the door to the plastic box, he wanted to run and dive under her bed; she needed to pay for such gross mistreatment. But the soreness between his shoulders made him move slowly and Brittany picked him up before he was two steps out.

"I'm sorry, Lucky." Brittany kissed his nose. "I know you hated that."

Jasper closed his eyes and sighed. *Then why did you do it?*

Chapter 15

OR SEVERAL DAYS AFTER THE VISIT TO the vet, Jasper felt drained, content to curl in the bay window where the sun reached in with glowing fingers in the late morning. He tried to stay suspicious and detached, but when Brittany made a determined effort to win him back with chin-scratching and tuna, he had no resistance.

Then she approached him with a leash with a small harness attached.

"Hi, Lucky." She sat down beside him and rubbed his head. Nathan stood in front of them, smiling and bouncing with excitement. Jasper studied him. *What's going on?*

"I've got a surprise." She held up the leash and let him smell it.

It didn't smell like anything very strongly. Maybe there was a hint of old Joey, but mostly it smelled like leather, like the family used for shoes and belts.

Brittany searched his face. "Want to go outside?"

She pulled the straps of the harness around him and started to fasten one of the buckles. He struggled.

"Here, Nathan, help me hold him." She gripped Jasper with one hand just above his shoulders and the other hand lower down his back.

"See where my hands are? Don't squeeze too tight, just hold him there when he tries to move," she said, nodding her head at Nathan.

Nathan carefully placed his hands next to Brittany's while Jasper writhed and tried to wiggle free. Brittany wrapped the straps in place so he was bound around his chest in front of his legs and behind them. She fastened the buckles and picked up the other end of the leash.

"Okay, Lucky." She stood up. "Let's go for a walk!"

Jasper stared at her, appalled. *You're not serious.*

She tugged gently on the leash. He rolled over and began clawing at the leather strap. *No way I'm going outside on a leash like some goofball dog.*

She released the pressure and Jasper stayed on his back for a few seconds, waiting to see if she was really giving up. He rolled back to his stomach.

"Doesn't like it," Nathan said.

Clever boy.

Brittany shrugged. "He will."

The next few minutes were a contest of wills. Brittany took a few steps and tugged on the leash. Jasper yowled a protest and rolled, grappling with the leash, trying to gnaw it into pieces. She stopped pulling and he stopped struggling.

Finally, after a quiet spell, she snatched him up into her arms. Jasper struggled, harder as he realized they were headed toward the front door.

"Ow!" she said when he scratched her. "Quick, Nathan. Open it."

Once outside, Brittany ran to the grass and dumped him. Nathan ran with his thumping steps behind them.

The outside air was tantalizing. He stopped battling the leash and stood up to look around. There was the faint tang of autumn in the air; a few bold leaves beginning to touch the trees with their last vivid glory. He thought he saw the pale outline of the moon in the bright sky but even as he stared, she was silent, unresponsive. *Probably because the sun is so strong*, he told himself, and tried hard to believe it.

He scanned the yard and street. One man, wiry as a cricket, pounded down the street in his running shorts and tee shirt, staring straight ahead. Two women approached from the other direction, one pushing a baby carriage. The occasional car hummed near and whooshed by.

"Come on, Lucky." Brittany tugged on the leash. "Let's walk."

Little by little, they moved across the yard toward the street, Brittany and Nathan nudging and cajoling and Jasper struggling to twist free of the leash. The three finally reached the smooth curve of the curb.

"Okay." Brittany stopped. "Give him a treat now, Nathan."

Nathan dug into his pocket and pulled out a packaged morsel. He held it out to the cat.

Jasper sniffed at it then backed away. He had his limits. *The day I eat from someone's hand will be the day I start barking.*

"Put it down," Brittany said.

Nathan placed the treat carefully just in front of Jasper. Jasper crouched and devoured the tidbit.

"Now," Brittany said. "We're going to go see Mrs. Bradley."

"Mrs. Bradley?" Nathan said.

"I told you about her. She lives two streets over. She has the beautiful white cat I told you about. Remember?"

Nathan shook his head.

Brittany took a few steps. "Well, that's where we're going."

The journey was long and tedious.

Jasper kept hoping that Brittany would give up and release him from the leash but the girl had her plan and she wasn't going to deviate. They would take a few steps, then Jasper would roll and twist and rub against the ground trying to pull off the straps. Nathan would pick him up and set him on his feet or Brittany would pick him up and carry him a few steps, speaking seriously to him about his behavior.

Finally they approached a familiar series of yards. Jasper looked around and spotted the frosty-haired woman, kneeling in front of her shrubs. Brittany stopped walking. Nathan dug in his pocket for another treat that he positioned in front of Jasper.

"Hello, Mrs. Bradley," Brittany called out.

The frosty-haired woman stood up and pulled off her gardening gloves.

"Well, hello there, Brittany." She studied Nathan. "You must be Nathan."

The boy nodded.

"I've heard a lot of good things about you." She smiled at him. He stared at her and stepped behind Brittany.

"And you!" The frosty-haired woman squatted down to rub Jasper's head. "Look at you! Sleek and shiny as a show cat!"

Brittany smiled. "He's doing good, isn't he?"

"He looks marvelous." The woman looked at Brittany. "You've been taking wonderful care of him."

Please take this thing off of me. Please, Jasper implored the frosty-haired woman. Surely she could see how undignified and unnatural it was for a cat to wear a harness.

"How's he taking to the leash?" the woman asked.

Brittany worked her mouth. "He'll get used to it."

"Sure he will." The woman scratched Jasper's chin and cheeks. He purred. She patted his belly. "Look how fat you are."

"He likes you," Nathan said.

"Well," the frosty-haired woman said, "I fed him once or twice when he had nobody else."

The faint jingle of a choke collar shocked Jasper into standing, rigid and alert. It was Max trotting on a leash beside the purposeful stride of the big man. Jasper relaxed and Brittany picked him up.

Max stopped and barked. "Jasper?"

The big man stopped and squinted. "You've got to be kidding."

"Hello, Frank," the frosty-haired woman said.

"Edna," the big man said. "What have you done to that cat?"

"Not a thing. Doesn't he look healthy and wonderful? Brittany is doing a splendid job taking care of him."

The big man took a few steps closer. "He looks like a little pig."

Look who's talking, Jasper thought.

"He does not." Brittany face was flushed and she squeezed Jasper close. "Maybe you shouldn't bring that dog so close."

"Frank," the frosty-haired woman warned. "He looks wonderful. Don't you remember how skinny he was? When he was attacked here in my yard?" She gave the big angry man a meaningful look.

To Jasper's amazement, the big man coughed and ducked his head. "Yeah, yeah, I guess you're right. But Max is a lot better behaved now. He doesn't chase cats anymore."

"How do you like the leash there, big fella?" Max said, and chuckled.

"Oh, go find a bone," Jasper said.

Nathan was staring at Max with a rapt expression. He whispered to Brittany. She shook her head. He whispered again. She sighed.

"Does your dog bite?" Brittany nodded toward Max.

"Only little boys with dark hair and blue tee shirts," the big man said. He didn't seem nearly so angry as he always had before, but there was still that rough unpredictable edge to him that made Jasper nervous.

Nathan looked down at his blue tee shirt, then back up at the man.

The man laughed, a short choppy laugh that sounded like a bark. "No, he won't bite. Go ahead and pet him." He kneeled on one knee and thumped Max's side.

Nathan extended one hand very slowly toward the dog who sniffed at it.

"He's all right, Max," Jasper said. Brittany wasn't holding him quite so tightly. They were all watching Nathan patting the dog's head with a soft careful hand.

"Hey, will you do me a favor?" Jasper said to Max. "When I take off, chase me, okay?"

The dog sighed. "Do I have to? I'll get in trouble. I'm not supposed to chase cats anymore. Go figure." He rubbed his head against Nathan's hand and gave him a friendly smile.

"I just can't take it," Jasper said. He coiled and jumped from the girl's arms toward the back yard.

"Lucky!" Brittany said.

Jasper ran hard around the corner of the garage toward the back of the house, dragging the leash behind him like a useless second tail. He got to the back yard and stood for a moment, savoring his freedom. There was a faint high-pitched noise from the kitchen window. He walked closer and saw Precious' snarling face.

How rude.

He stepped closer to the window.

"I have my own person now," he spoke to the spitting white cat through the glass. "There's no need to be so hateful."

His words had no effect on her; her tail stayed almost as big as she was.

Brittany ran around the house, Nathan close behind her.

"Lucky!" she said. "What are you doing?"

He lifted up a front paw, licked it and rubbed his face. He was tired. This leash business was terribly hard work. The children approached him slowly, from opposite sides and he made no attempt to escape.

Brittany reached him first and she picked up the end of the leash.

"It's okay, Lucky," she said. "That dog's gone now. I know he scared you."

It's not Max who scares me, Jasper thought as she picked him up. *It's your crazy ideas: baths, vets, leashes. What's next?*

"How about a glass of tea?" The frosty-haired woman stood by her back door, beckoning the children inside. Brittany tied the end of Jasper's leash to the same railing where the big man had tied Max so many days ago. Jasper slumped to the ground in shame.

"She's so beautiful," Brittany said from inside the kitchen.

Jasper couldn't help looking and saw the two children sitting on the floor while Precious paraded around the kitchen. Nathan reached out a tentative hand and the silky white cat evaded his touch and stood up on her hind legs, her front paws braced against the frosty-haired woman's leg. The children laughed.

The woman smiled and set the glasses of tea down on the table. She bent over and lifted Precious so the two touched nose to nose, then turned her to hold her in the circle of her arms like an infant. The woman gently rocked the cat who purred and blinked at the world like a rock-solid favorite child.

Finally, Brittany and Nathan trudged home, mostly carrying Jasper as he still refused to walk more than a few resistant steps in response to the pressure of the leash. Rather than drag him, they carried him, first Brittany, then Nathan for a brief spell, then Brittany again. Jasper searched the sky and trees from the jerky cradle of their arms, thinking of Hank.

Finally, when they were back to Brittany's front yard, he heard a familiar voice.

"I've never seen a cat on a leash before," Hank said, from a tall sprawling oak.

"There's a reason for that," Jasper said. "Where have you been?"

"I've been around, just like always. Why don't you come out anymore?"

"Oh," Jasper said as they walked up the steps to the front porch. "I've been busy inside."

"I'm worried about you, Jasper," Hank's voice was fading as they walked inside the front door. "You're all numb and blank."

"Nonsense!" Jasper jumped to the ground and tried to make a run upstairs.

Brittany stepped on the end of the leash and caught him up short. The harness chafed around his body. She unbuckled the straps and he was free to gallop up the stairs. He crept under Brittany's bed to rest and reflect.

What did he mean, all numb and blank? Jasper wondered.

Chapter 16

HE DAYS WENT BY, getting shorter with the
approaching autumn, and Jasper's life began to take on
the quality of a foggy but comfortable dream.
Nighttime was the most difficult. All the humans slept
their heavy, long sleep, while Jasper prowled the house, checking the
windows for a glimpse of the moon outside the flat pale belly of the
ceiling. It had been so long since he'd had a vision that he wondered
if it was over. *Maybe I'll never have another one. Maybe since I have a
home, I don't need to have them anymore.*

He thought he saw Hank one night, a mottled flash of wings
diving though the back yard, but the big bird never came close to the
sliding glass door where Jasper sat for hours, staring into the darkness.

He would dream of the moon, in the long lonely stretches during
the day when Brittany was back at school and at night while all of
them slept. In his dreams, the moon looked deeply sad and disap-
pointed, and he would awaken with his heart thumping and that
awful empty feeling in his stomach. He would hurry to the bowl of

dry food left out for him and crunch away, but the empty feeling persisted.

Then morning would come and with it, the harsh hum of the can opener and the bowl of luscious moist lumps. He ate until the bowl was clean, regardless of whether he was hungry. His stomach had swelled into a hard round ball that swung from side to side when he walked. His balance was a little off, but what did he care? *All I ever wanted was a home, to eat regularly, to be loved by a human.*

The man ignored him, Cole avoided him, Nathan adored him, and Brittany treated him like a second little brother. The tall woman liked him more than she allowed the others to see, and slipped bits of meat to him while she prepared meals. Life would have been perfect if he'd been allowed outside on his own but Brittany hovered over him and anticipated his breaks for the outside. The only times she took him outside, she strapped him into the harness and wanted him to walk along beside her like an obedient idiot dog.

Then one morning, he slipped out, just behind the man's heavy steps before the door slammed shut. It was morning, with crisp air and damp grass and the sun soft and smiling. He tasted the air and quivered with pleasure. The cool cheek of the earth was alive beneath the smooth pads of his feet. Cold weather was on its way; last time he'd been out, he'd felt the hot, burdened breath of summer.

It wasn't natural to always stay inside a box, even a pleasant, warm box with plenty of food and affection like Brittany's house. He looked up at the clean blue face of the sky.

Hello.

And it seemed as though the sky smiled and nodded back when a breeze brushed him lightly like a friendly cat. The birds twittered and whistled to themselves and each other, and he could hear the drone of cars in the street approach and fade away.

Then behind him, he felt and heard the flat thumping footsteps of Nathan.

"Wucky!" The boy slowed down as he approached. He squatted down to pick Jasper up and the cat danced away from him. *Not just yet.*

Nathan straightened and took a few steps after him. When he bent down, Jasper jumped just out of his reach.

"Wucky!" Nathan put his fists on his hips. "Come here!"

Jasper walked, in no particular hurry, through the neighbors' yards. There was that bubbling creek close by that he wanted to explore. *Then I'll be ready to come back in.*

The jingle of a dog collar startled him and he bounded a short distance before he recognized Max's voice.

"Jasper!" Max sounded a little strained.

He stopped and took a look back. It was Max all right but he was not alone. The big man held him tight on the leash while Max pranced and whined.

"Relax, Max," the man said. "Just take it easy."

The big man, angry or not, still made Jasper nervous. *Without Brittany or the frosty-haired woman around to protect him, who knows what he might do?* Max had been friendly since the fire, but always alone. The big man might order him to attack. Animals under the direct order of humans were always slightly suspect.

Jasper loped through several yards, eager to build some distance between himself and the others. Then he noticed a rock ahead with something on top that was rounded and dark, something with a dull shine. He approached slowly, his old outside instincts in play, tasting the air for some clues about the dark lump.

The breeze was going the wrong way for him to get an easy handle on the scent, so he stood for a few long moments, listening intently, watching for movement. When Nathan landed one heavy hand on his back, Jasper sprinted to the rock to take a closer look.

The dark lump coiled, and opened his mouth wide. The inside of the snake's mouth gaped white against the dull black of his body. His mouth stayed open as he hissed.

"Stay away," the snake said. "I'll hurt you."

Jasper stopped. His heart swelled with fear, nearly stopping, than began beating as if it had already made the decision to run and was leaving him behind.

"Sorry!" He scrambled back a few steps. There was no negotiating with snakes. "Didn't mean to wake you!"

Nathan saw the snake and stepped toward it, his mouth a soft *O* of wonder. Jasper yowled in warning, but Nathan stretched a slow hand toward the black coil.

"Don't you know who I am?" The snake hissed harder, jaws open, mouth deadly white, and tightened to strike.

Jasper jumped at the boy, claws slashing. *Stay away! Get back!*

Nathan screamed as Jasper hit him and raked his claws across his arm, but he fell back. The snake swayed his head a little but stayed on the rock. Jasper chased the boy until he fell down.

Nathan sat up and held his arm, his face contorted by tears. Jasper rubbed against him and the boy shrank away from his touch.

"Wucky," he said to Jasper. "You hurt me."

But I had to. Don't you see?

"You all right there, son?" It was the big man, still holding Max tight with the leash, watching from the next yard.

Nathan shook his head and cried without making any noise.

I'm sorry. Jasper tried again to rub the boy but he pushed at Jasper with one hand.

"Go 'way, Wucky."

The big man came closer, Max gasping by his side. Jasper ran a prudent ways away, toward a tree that looked easy enough for a fat cat to climb.

"What happened, Jasper?" Max said. "Why'd you jump at him like that? We saw you do it."

"Didn't you see the snake?" Jasper said.

"Snake?" Max's ears went up. "You saw a snake? Boy, I love to play with snakes. Where is he?"

"You don't want to play with this one, Max," Jasper said.

"I'll be the judge of that." Max bounced up and down.

"Where is he?"

Jasper shook his head. *Doesn't anybody around here know a bad snake when they see him?*

"I do." It was Hank, stealthy as ever.

"Hank!" Jasper said. "Where have you been? How long have you been there? You saw the snake?"

Hank nodded. He cocked his head. "Did you know that was going to happen? That the boy was going to be in danger?"

Jasper shook his head. "Not a clue."

The big owl studied Jasper with his sharp yellow eyes until Jasper felt itchy and uncomfortable.

"Is he okay?" Hank asked.

The two of them looked over at Nathan, still sitting, head down. The big man squatted to examine his arm. Max sniffed at the boy.

"Pretty nice set of scratches you got there," the big man said and dropped Nathan's arm. "You're a lucky fella. That cat was taking care of you."

Nathan shook his head hard.

"You think I'm kidding with you. You know what kind of snake that was?" The big man glanced toward the rock. The black snake had slipped out of sight.

The boy squinted at him.

"It was a cottonmouth. Poisonous as all get out." The big man nodded toward the oozing red scratches on Nathan's arm and shook his head. "We better get you home."

The big man put his hands on his knees and pushed to stand. He offered a hand to Nathan. Nathan rolled over, hopped to his feet, and took off running his flat-footed gait.

"Hey!" the big man said, then he looked at Max and shrugged. "Guess he was ready to go."

"I probably need to get back with Nathan," Jasper said to Hank, then began trotting after the boy, careful to swing a wide arc around Max and the big man.

"Jasper?" Hank called after him.

Jasper, still feeling Hank's scalding look on his face, picked up his speed.

———

"Nathan!" the tall woman called.

Jasper arrived in the yard before Nathan, and he greeted the woman with relief.

"Well, there you are!" The woman put her hands on her hips. "You snuck out, didn't you? I'll bet you took Nathan with you." She looked behind Jasper.

"Momma," Nathan said, breathless as he walked up to the tall woman. He held out his arm to her.

"What happened?" The woman's eyes narrowed. "Those look like cat scratches." She looked at Jasper, her eyes suddenly small and cool with suspicion.

"Did you do this?" She asked Jasper as if she expected an answer. She looked back at Nathan. "Did Lucky do this?"

Nathan nodded. "Wucky is a good cat. Help me."

The woman shook her head and when she spoke, her voice was hollow and distant. "I don't think so. These are terrible scratches. Did you do something to hurt Lucky, Nathan?"

Nathan shook his head no.

"Let's get inside, Nathan." She turned to the door.

Nathan shuffled, his steps slow with fatigue.

The woman herded the boy inside and Jasper slipped around them into the kitchen. He sat and looked at her with hopeful expectance. *Time for a snack? A treat for being such a good cat?*

The tall woman lifted Jasper and deposited him back outside the door.

"I'm sorry, Lucky." She spoke to him through the screen. "I can't have a cat that's going to hurt my children."

Bewildered, Jasper sat. *What did she mean? I wasn't trying to hurt him.* He sat and wondered when Brittany would be home. Brittany would understand, and would explain it to the woman.

"She thinks you scratched Nathan on purpose. Just for meanness." Hank spoke from a nearby pine.

"Meanness?" Jasper said. "How could she think that?"

Hank shrugged. "She doesn't know any better. She doesn't know about the snake and he won't be able to explain it."

"But how could she think I would do that?" Frustration flooded Jasper like a sudden, drenching rainstorm.

Hank said nothing.

"It's not true, Hank. Surely she's got to realize that. How wrong she is." Jasper paced. "It will get straightened out when Brittany comes home."

But when Brittany got home later, as the sun was leaning low in the sky, she ran inside too quickly for Jasper to approach her.

He waited while the sky grew shadowed, then dark, and the fresh cool of the evening settled in the neighborhood like an old friend visiting. He watched the moon rise, opaque and enticing as ever.

"Hello?" Jasper said.

There was no reply. His stomach began to rumble; he hadn't eaten since early morning. His gut began to ache with the old familiar pain. Hunger and something else.

He stared at the moon, all his frustration and anger suddenly focused on her. She with her ripe well-fed curves, her simple words that made it all so seem so easy, so inevitable, so orderly.

"It's not fair!" he said, and it came out in an anguished yowl. "I did the right thing. I saved that boy from a bad snakebite."

The moon said nothing. The wind tickled the trees and they whispered to themselves, to each other, about his poor behavior.

"Are you going to help me? Set things straight? Of course not. You're not in the business of making dreams come true; you just like to sit up there in your soft cushioned sky and order us around down here."

He looked hard at the moon.

I hate you, he thought. *Do you know that? Do you care?*

Chapter 17

ASPER SLEPT FITFULLY, curled in a tight ball under the deck at the back of Brittany's house. Small sounds woke him: creaks from the floorboards inside the house, someone coughing, the water rushing to fill then drain from the washing machine, the splash and dim gurgle of a toilet flushing.

He kept waiting for Brittany to come out. To call for him and gather him up, pet him and fuss over him like a lost child. It was considerably colder than when he'd first gone in the house and, in the regulated air inside, his coat hadn't thickened like it normally would have.

He lay under the deck and watched the faint cool fingers of the moon reach beneath the boards of the deck. He closed his eyes and tightened the curl of his body for warmth and dozed.

The image in his mind flashed sudden and terrible. It was Precious, the frosty-haired woman's pampered white cat, dashing into the street in front of an oblivious Ford Mustang. Jasper opened his eyes and shook his head. *Not going to happen. Just wishful thinking.*

He settled himself down again and closed his eyes. The image flashed again, insistent and vivid.

No. He squeezed his eyes shut and conjured an image of his breakfast bowl, the moist, fragrant clumps of food. *I'm through with helping anybody else. What good has it done me? I'd probably get myself hit.*

"Jasper?" Hank's voice was above the deck.

Jasper didn't answer Hank but his eyes opened wide in the shadows of the deck. An ant trickled across his paw and he bit at it. He tried to ignore the faint but distinct, wrong feeling in his gut. *Not my responsibility. I'm just taking care of me. That's all. Nobody helps me. I'm tired of trying to help everybody else. Maybe if I don't do it, I'll quit seeing the things once and for all.*

"Jasper, it doesn't work like that," Hank said. "Talk to me. You're making a mistake."

Jasper closed his eyes and thought hard about Brittany. Another image flooded his mind. In the vision, Brittany stood beside the frosty-haired woman who was kneeling like she was planting again in her yard. Except the woman was shaking and crying and Brittany had a hand on the kneeling woman's shoulder and both looked very serious and very sad.

Uck! This is awful. Jasper jumped up and started to run in the cool moonlight. He had to keep moving. Just so he wouldn't doze and see those terrible pictures.

"Jasper!" Hank said.

Jasper didn't slow down.

———

Jasper ran until he reached his old home, the fort in the woods. The familiar uneven lines of it made his heart hurt. It looked pathetic to him, shabbier than he remembered. Home for an outcast.

He climbed the tree, more slowly than he used to with his extra belly, but eventually he gained the top. He headed toward the dark corner where the branch grew close over the roof, where he'd always slept.

There was someone in his spot. A wiry-haired creature, about his size, with a sharp white face and a long pink tail, crouched and growled. It was a possum.

"Hello," Jasper said.

"What do you want?" the possum snarled. "Get out of here."

Why was it that so many creatures had no manners to speak of?

"I think there's been a misunderstanding," Jasper said, sitting down.

"That's right," the possum said, pulling his lips back to show an impressive set of large sharp fangs. "You don't understand that this is my place and you're not welcome."

He lunged at Jasper who jumped back just in time. The cat stood on the edge of the roof, trying to strike a threatening pose. He flattened his ears and made his tail as big as possible.

"This is my home," Jasper said. "I've been gone for a little while, but it really belongs to me."

"Oh yeah?" the possum said. "Well, kick me out then, if it's yours."

He rushed toward Jasper, his face distorted. Jasper thought briefly of Precious and how much he'd like to get her and the possum together since they had the same approach to other creatures. He made his way down the tree as quickly as his bulk and dignity would allow.

Jasper walked away and his stomach rumbled. He thought of the chicken place. It was a fair distance, and as he glanced at the suggestion of light at the horizon, he decided against it. *It'll be light soon and I'll go to Brittany's house to patch things up.* For the time being, the thick tangle of leggy, prickly bushes felt like the right place to wait for the morning.

He waited and dozed, and kept fighting the image of Precious and the car that came back again and again like a persistent horsefly. Or at least that was how Jasper tried to think of it. *It's not my problem.*

I'm not going to do a thing but ignore it.

When the sun finally pushed her dazzling face into view, Jasper was exhausted, edgy and irritable from lack of sleep. He stretched briefly and trotted toward Brittany's house.

He got there in time to see Chloe and Joey crunching on dry food.

"Well, look who's here," Chloe turned her head toward him and licked her lips. "Mr. Favorite Cat looks like he got kicked out."

Joey glanced at him and kept eating.

She took a few steps away and began to groom herself.

"What happened, Mangy?" She licked one paw and scrubbed her face. "Did you poop on somebody's bed?"

"Ha!" Joey laughed. "I remember when you did that, Chloe. I thought—"

He stopped short when he saw the evil look Chloe directed at him.

"I meant to say, I did that," Joey said. "It's how I ended up out here."

"It's all a big misunderstanding," Jasper sat down and tried not to look at the dry food.

"Misunderstanding?" Chloe blinked. "Right." She yawned. "I heard them talking about what you did to the younger boy."

"I saved him from a snakebite! That's what I did," Jasper said, his tail twitching.

"Yes, dear, I'm sure you did." She glanced at the back door. "If I were you, I'd skedaddle before anybody comes out. They think you lost patience with Nathan and scratched him."

"No!" Jasper said and stood.

The back door creaked open and Brittany stepped out.

"Lucky!" she said and ran toward him.

"Brittany!" The tall woman stood in the doorway and her voice had a warning note. Brittany stopped short, tears on her face.

"I told you, I think we need to let Lucky find another home."

"But he doesn't have another home." Brittany shifted her feet.

"He can't stay here if I have to worry about him hurting Nathan, honey," the woman's voice softened. "Now come inside. It will be easier for him to leave if you pretend he's already gone."

Jasper trotted to Brittany and rubbed against her legs. *Surely she can see that I wouldn't scratch Nathan on purpose. Come on, Brittany, you know I would only have done something like that for a good reason. Think, girl.*

Brittany squatted and rubbed his head.

"Brittany." The woman's voice was hard again.

Brittany shook her head, and covered her face with her hands. When she ran into the house, Jasper sat down to wait.

He waited until the fear and frustration bubbled up inside him so that he thought he might explode with the pressure of it. He began to run.

He ran to the woods and huddled beside a big fallen limb. Breathing hard, he tried to collect his thoughts. He felt like he'd been thrown in water again, only this time cold, rushing water that was too deep for him to get a foothold on the bottom.

How could this happen? All I tried to do was save the boy.

He looked up at the fierce blazing face of the sun. He searched the sky for the pale outline of the moon. He looked around for Hank.

He shook his head and sat in the grass and tried to think.

———

He sat by the log for a long time, trying to clear his jumbled thoughts. A slight thump on the log made him tense, ready to fight or run.

"Jasper?" It was Hank, of course.

He raised his head and looked at the owl.

"Precious has gotten out," Hank said. "We've got to hurry."

Jasper shook his head. "No."

"No what?" Hank said. "We've got to hurry or we won't get there in time."

"I'm not going," Jasper said, despite the sick feeling in his gut.

"Not going?" Hank blinked his big yellow eyes. "But you have to go."

"No," Jasper said. "I don't. I'm finished with it."

"But why?" Hank twisted his head toward the neighborhood houses. "Something bad will happen if you don't."

"Something bad happened when I did!" Jasper said. "Only it happened to me so I guess that doesn't really count."

Hank shook his head. "I'm not sure I follow you, but if we're going to go, we have to go now."

"I told you," Jasper said. "I'm not going."

Hank looked at him, and the poisonous feeling in Jasper began to writhe and shape itself into something with a voice.

You don't have to do anything you don't want to do. And what if something does happen to Precious? The frosty-haired woman has always liked you.

"Get out of here," said Jasper and he snarled. "Leave me alone."

Hank lifted his wings and the light click of his talons on the dry bark of the log was the only sound he made. Then he was gone.

You're doing the right thing, the noxious voice in Jasper said. *You're taking care of yourself for once. How about something to eat?*

Jasper trotted the distance to the fast-food chicken place, trying to remember the schedule. *Is morning the best time? Or is midday better?*

The long scream of brakes that echoed through the neighborhood reached his ears as a faint, faraway sound. He never heard the small thud.

Chapter 18

ASPER FOUND A BAG of half-eaten chicken by the road near the chicken place and ate his fill of the cold, heavy meat. His belly full, he took a short nap then headed back to the neighborhood. The late afternoon sun was nowhere to be seen; the face of the sky had turned an impassive gray that cast a hard, colorless light. Stringy and forlorn, the leafless trees stretched overhead toward the sky like naked newborns, unwilling to accept the cold conspiracy of winter.

His way back took him by the frosty-haired woman's house and he heard voices in the back yard. One of them sounded like Brittany. He trotted closer to take a look.

They had their backs to him, but he could see the frosty-haired woman, kneeling on the ground, like she did so often working in the yard, and Brittany standing close beside her, one hand on the woman's shoulder.

As he got closer, he could see that the woman was shaking with sobs, her head down.

"It was my fault," she said. "I opened the door for that magazine salesman and out she went."

"It wasn't your fault." Brittany patted the woman's shoulder.

"It was," the woman said. "I was too slow." She took a deep breath. "I just can't believe she's gone. It was so quick."

A nasty crawling feeling began to tickle inside Jasper's mind. *No. It didn't really happen.*

"I know." Brittany nodded. "That's how it was with Alicia. We were running a race and I was showing off and winning like I always did." She shook her head. "I can't remember if I heard the car or not. But it felt like my fault. If I hadn't been running so fast and proving that I could beat her..." She shrugged.

The frosty-haired woman looked up into Brittany's face. "Oh, child, you mustn't think that."

"But that's what happened." Brittany's voice went high and thin until it broke. "And if it wasn't my fault, then whose fault was it?"

The woman wrapped an arm around the girl and hugged her.

Brittany wiped her face with the back of her hand and reached into her pocket. She pulled out a lumpy handkerchief and carefully unfolded it.

"Here," she said to the woman. "This is for you."

It was the small ivory cat from the white table in Brittany's room.

The woman accepted it with both hands. "Isn't it beautiful?"

"It belonged to Alicia and I always thought it looked like Precious. I was going to give it to you anyway."

The woman's face crumpled and she brought a hand to her mouth. "Thank you, dear."

Jasper moved to the edge of the yard, where he could hide in the shrubbery and watch what happened without being seen. *Not now*, he told himself. *Not the right time to approach either one of them.*

He picked his way through the azaleas until he was close enough to see their faces. In front of the frosty-haired woman was a matted white lump. The breeze shifted his way and he caught the terrible, unmistakable smell of death.

He recoiled. *No!*

Jasper shook his head and squinted. It was Precious, but it wasn't. Whatever had made Precious the beautiful ill-tempered cat she had been, was gone. On the ground was a lifeless cat-shaped heap of body and fur.

Something inside Jasper moaned. *You could have prevented it! No! It wasn't my fault.*

The voices in his head screamed and raged and Jasper had to run to keep from listening. The wind began to blow harder, snapping leaves and twigs through the air, against his sides. The face of the sky grew darker, more smudged and Jasper didn't look once for the moon.

He didn't slow down until he was almost to the fort. The possum was coming from the opposite direction, slower than a cat, even a fat, out-of-condition cat. Jasper tensed.

The possum sneered, his nose twitching. "Well, look who's back."

Jasper attacked the possum, jumping on his back with his claws outstretched, trying to find his neck through the coarse, wiry fur. The possum rolled and the two of them snarled and scratched and bit as they tumbled.

For the first time in his life, Jasper fought with no intention of running. Every time the possum bit him, something in him smiled. Every bite and scratch felt like punishment that he deserved. *What difference does it make?* And so he fought until the possum raked his eye so that it scalded and burned like he'd walked into a flame.

He screamed. He couldn't see anything out of that eye and the pain was overwhelming. In a frenzy, he lunged at the possum and bit deeply into his leg.

The possum squealed and, when Jasper released his grip, scurried off through the woods. Jasper sat on the forest floor and waited for his breathing to settle and for the relentless pain in his eye to lessen.

The pain didn't lessen, and after a few minutes, he began to feel weak and dizzy. He settled down on the ground to rest while the wind whipped around him like a scolding mother.

A picture flashed across his mind. Hank, his wing bloodied, feathers askew, was on the ground and the big man was walking toward him, shovel in his hand.

Jasper shuddered. *Hank is in trouble. Got to help him.* He stood up and started to walk the familiar path to the neighborhood. Only it looked entirely unfamiliar with just one eye.

Don't do it! The shrill ugly voice in his head screamed at him, but the sound was fading. But the voice in the center of him answered. *Shut up. I have to do this.*

His balance was off and he had to stop a few times but finally he stumbled into the soft grass of the big man's back yard.

Hank was at the very back of the yard, in the thin shadowy edge of the woods. He was indeed on the ground.

"Hank!" Jasper said.

"Jasper?" Hank's voice was tight with pain. "What are you doing here?"

As he got closer, Jasper turned his good eye so that he could see Hank. He looked bad. His wing was streaked with a heavy dark blotch and he was holding it at a funny angle, like he couldn't fold it flat against his body. There was a bitter, sharp smell about him that Jasper didn't like.

"What's wrong with your eye?" Hank asked.

"Little fight. What happened to you?" Jasper said. "Can you get off the ground?" He turned his head so he could look toward the house. No sign of the big man yet.

Hank shook his head. "I tried to stop Precious and didn't keep a good eye on the car."

Jasper's heart thudded as he looked at the big owl, broken and defenseless on the ground. "We've got to get you somewhere safe."

They both heard it at the same time: the jingle of a dog collar. The lean, deadly Doberman was trotting toward them, sniffing at the bottoms of the substantial trees.

Jasper's heart seized with fright, then bounced like a hard rubber ball inside the walls of his chest. He flattened himself in the grass, although it hurt, and willed the dog to just keep moving. But the wind had picked up, dancing and gusting enough to carry their scent to the dog.

The Doberman raised his head and sniffed. He was only about the distance of one back yard away. He started his muscular trot again, this time toward the street.

Brittany was walking down the street with Nathan, a slow speculative walk. She was stopping every few steps and scanning the yards. Nathan walked slowly beside her, staring at the pavement directly in front of him, then up at the sky.

"Jasper?" Hank said.

"Shhhh," Jasper said.

"Do you see the little people?" Hank asked.

"Hank, we need to be quiet right now." Jasper kept his good eye on the dog.

Nathan stopped walking and cocked his head.

"I hear him!" Nathan said.

"Who?" Brittany kept walking, still searching.

"The owl," Nathan said. He looked in the big man's back yard and pointed.

"Come on, Nathan." Brittany still didn't look at him.

The Doberman approached the children. Nathan pulled his arm in to his body. Brittany froze.

"Don't move, Nathan," she said.

The boy began to back up, making a high-pitched humming sound. The Doberman stepped closer, sniffing at his belt.

Jasper sighed. *I'll never make it.* With effort, he got up and trotted toward the dog and the boy. He spoke, weakly at first then more loudly as he gained strength.

"Hey, lunkhead! I can smell you from here. Yeah, you, stinky!"

The dog jerked his head toward Jasper, and seeing him, forgot the boy. He began his springy trot toward Jasper.

"Wucky!" Nathan said.

"Lucky?" Brittany said.

"Bring it here, big guy! Let's see how tough you really are!" Jasper said.

The back door slammed and the big man stood like a misshapen oak, his face unreadable. He picked up a shovel leaning by the back door and began striding toward Jasper. *This is it, then.* Between the dog and the man, Jasper sat down. He took a deep breath and tasted all the ripe beauty of the air. He looked up at the sky and saw a break in the rushing dark face. The white curve of the moon hung in the sky like smoke, like a stubborn cloud.

"I've missed you," she said, although it was hard to hear her in the low grumbling thunder of the approaching storm.

The sound of her sweet voice was all Jasper needed. He waited for the dog and man and wondered who would reach him first.

The Doberman pranced closer, head high, lifting his quivering lip above the bone-white curves of his fangs. He kept coming, growling low, deep in his chest and the smell of him was strong, sharp with his excitement. Jasper could feel the thump of his feet on the ground all throughout his body, and hear the shrieks of Brittany and Nathan fade as the thumps grew stronger. He came so close that Jasper could hear the hoarse rustle of his breath and feel the hot sour sweep of it against his face.

Jasper closed his eyes and tried not to cringe. With any luck at all, the dog would be quick. One quick snap of the jaws on his neck and it would be over. Lightning cracked not too far away and the dog stopped and stiffened just long enough.

The man lifted the shovel and stepped between him and the Doberman. Jasper smelled coffee and dirt and the faint charred smell of smoke. *Funny*, he thought. *Hank and I saved his life from that fire and he doesn't even know it. And now he's going to kill me.*

The big man swung the shovel at the dog.

"Get out of here," he said. "Go on home."

The Doberman ducked and circled to approach from another angle. He lunged close and Jasper heard his jaws snap and felt a hot gust of air brush his face. Thunder rumbled again, closer.

"Don't make me hurt you, now," the big man said. "Go on." He stomped, and the dog stopped. The man dug the shovel in the ground and lifted up a healthy clump of his own luxurious grass. He swung it hard at the dog and it thumped on the Doberman's side.

The dog yelped lightly, took a few stutter steps then broke into a run.

The big man leaned over Jasper, who closed his eyes and waited to feel the shovel on his own bruised head. *Be quick about it. Please.*

The man's fingers were surprisingly soft.

"Something got ahold of you, didn't it?" the man said. "You might just lose that eye."

Jasper opened his eyes and turned his head to look at him. The big man's eyes were a rich dark brown.

"Lucky!" Brittany stood trembling above him, Nathan beside her, his eyes enormous. "Is he all right?"

The big man dropped to one knee beside the cat. "He might make it. I'm not sure about that owl."

"What owl?" Brittany said. "Where?" Nathan nodded, unsurprised.

"He's out there in the back of the yard. Got a hurt wing, I think. How about if you go tell your mom to call Animal Control or the Nature Museum? There's some place around here where they take care of birds like that. I'll get this boy to the vet."

The children stood staring at Jasper.

"Well?" The man looked at them. "What are you waiting for?"

Brittany started to run, then slowed to match Nathan's slower pace. She reached out a hand and the boy took it.

"That boy next door used to call you Jasper, didn't he?" The man leaned close and Jasper could feel himself falling into the soft furred edges of unconsciousness. Lightning cracked again, hard and close by and the sound of it forced Jasper to his feet.

I need to see Hank. Make sure he's okay.

With all the strength he had, Jasper began an unsteady walk toward the back of the yard where he'd last seen the big bird. He looked overhead, trying to find the moon to tell her he was sorry. He'd failed in doing what she'd asked him to do, to take care of Hank.

The big owl still sat on the ground, blinking his eyes hard like he was trying to wake up.

"What can I do?" Jasper asked. "Just tell me."

"I'll be all right." Hank sighed. "Just need to rest a little."

Jasper sat down, his head spinning. *I'll just stay right here and protect him.*

"It's all right," the moon said.

Jasper looked up, through the outstretched arms of the trees and he could see only the fractious, tumbling clouds, smudged with storm dark.

"Everything is fine, Jasper. You've done well. Hank will be all right."

Even though he couldn't see her, her words touched the hot churning center of him and he sank to the ground.

"Where you think you're going, tough guy?" The man stooped beside him and carefully pulled the bottom of his shirt around the cat so he was cradled against the big belly. Rain began to fall gently, and the sweet cool feel of it on Jasper's head was indeed something precious.

Chapter 19

ASPER DIDN'T REMEMBER MUCH of the next few days. He had a dim recollection of going to the vet, mostly the strong frightening smells and perhaps the mantis man, his face hovering above like a low-hanging cloud. Or maybe he just imagined it in his pain and fever with all the other bad dreams. When he woke, he couldn't remember if Hank had died or if that had been part of the nightmares as well. Then he thought of the moon's words; that Hank would be fine, and the worst of the fear lifted a little.

The air smelled like hamburgers and French fries, rich with grease, with overtones of caustic mint and a hint of the old scorched smell of the fire. He was in the big man's house and he seemed to be resting in a small foam bed that smelled faintly of another cat.

"You finally waking up there, Mr. Jasper? Ready to take on the world again?" The man leaned over him, his meaty face relaxed, no longer angry. Jasper blinked, trying to get his bearings, but one eye, the one that had been scratched by the possum, was covered with something soft but nevertheless annoying. He reached up a paw to scratch it off and found a wide collar of hard plastic standing around his face that prevented him from rubbing his head with any of his paws. *What new form of human indignity was this?*

"You hungry?" The big man walked to the cabinet and pulled out a small can. Despite the collar, and the unfamiliar surroundings, and the dull itchiness in his eye, Jasper stood and stretched. Yes indeed, he was hungry.

He took a few tentative steps out of the bed, noticing that the wide collar interfered with his balance, and he certainly didn't like the way it limited his range of vision. He lifted his nose and tasted the air again, detecting another familiar smell.

"Thought you were never going to wake up." Max sprawled by the back door, which had an odd square flap in the bottom section.

"Hi, Max." Jasper wanted to be polite but the man had popped open the can that definitely smelled like tuna.

"Those kids have been here every day to see you." Max lifted his nose, catching wind of the tuna.

"Brittany and Nathan?" Standing up took a lot of effort, so Jasper sat on the cool, hard floor.

"That's what the big guy calls 'em." Max stood and came close enough to sniff at Jasper's collar. "What's that thing on your head?"

Jasper sighed. "Ask the big guy."

Max gave him a long, assessing look, his ears pricked forward. "I just want to know one thing."

"What's that?" *What's the holdup with the tuna?* Jasper watched the broad bulk of the big man, who hummed as he squirted a small syringe of liquid into the bowl and stirred it carefully.

"What were you thinking when you took on Brutus? If the big guy hadn't been around, he would have killed you. That dog's serious."

Jasper reached up to scratch his eye, forgetting about the plastic. "I don't know. I guess I wasn't really thinking." The memories of the day rushed over him and he shivered with the thought of how close he had been to death. "Did you see it? Where were you?"

Max shook his head and shuffled to stand beside the big man. "I was right here in the kitchen. When the big guy saw the owl out back, he locked me up in here. Guess he was afraid I'd give Hank a hard time."

"Hank? What about Hank?" Jasper took a few steps toward the dog. "Have you seen him? Is he okay?"

Max shrugged. "Haven't seen him. Some people came and took him away in a big box. They were pretty careful about it. I think they said he would be all right." He gnawed on his front paw. "You can look for him yourself, soon as you feel up to it. I gotta figure out how I'm gonna explain it to the other dogs that you're living here. Think you could keep that kind of low-key?"

Jasper looked up at the big man, who was positioning a plastic mat on the floor by the foam cat bed. "You think he means for me to stay here?"

Max smiled, his tongue lolling. "He expects it." He nodded toward the door. "Know what that is?"

"A door?"

"Hah! No, genius, the little square, don't you see it? That's a cat door, and the big guy put it in special for you. So you can go in and out whenever the spirit moves you." He stood. "If I was the jealous type, like some cats I know, I'd be pitching a fit."

Jasper sat again, stunned with the idea of it. Who would have thought that the big angry man would offer the perfect home to a cat once chased from the yard like crabgrass or stray garbage? He watched the big man carefully carry a shallow bowl of fresh water to the mat.

Max looked up at the man, wagged his body and rubbed his big head against the man's leg. "I tried to tell you the big guy was all right. Hey, that tuna smells good."

"Forget it, Maxwell. You've already eaten. This is for Jasper." The man patted the dog's head.

"You gotta be kidding." Max sat back on his haunches and pawed the air. "Let's shake. Come on, boss, I was here first. And I can shake."

The big man blocked Max with his leg as he placed the bowl of tuna on the plastic floor mat beside the water. "Now go on, Max, or I'll have to put you outside."

"Hey!" Max whined. "Can't you see I'm starving here?"

"Don't worry," Jasper said, as he tasted the lovely pungency. "I'll leave some for you."

"Really?" Max perked up his ears and sat down.

"You bet," said Jasper.

The big man thumped Max on the side with affection. "That's a good boy. You'll get yours."

And Jasper had no doubt that he would.

ACKNOWLEDGMENTS

First, I thank the Creator, the One who started it all and continues the mystery.

My talented fellow writers Viki Cupaiuolo, Robert Herrin, Greg Lilly, Diana Renfro, and Jean Rowe, gave me feedback, friendship, and support from long before the first tentative scene of Jasper. This book would never have been written without them. My cats, Ripley and Emily, provided inspiration and the best sort of company for a writer at work: affectionate and silent.

I've been gifted with wonderful editors Amy Rogers and Frye Gaillard, who have welcomed me into the business of publishing with warmth and kindness.

My family is my bedrock; they continue to claim me with patience and love. I truly appreciate my family and friends willing to be honest first readers. I thank Anne Bowers and Marty Hedgpeth for being who they are and doing what they do. My tenth grade English teacher, Phyllis Gill, gave me attention and compassion when I sorely needed it; and I promised her a novel.

And finally, I thank my husband Doug, whose love, faith, and support have made all the difference.

NOVELLO FESTIVAL PRESS

Novello Festival Press, under the auspices of the Public Library of Charlotte and Mecklenburg County and through the publication of books of literary excellence, enhances the awareness of the literary arts, helps discover and nurture new literary talent, celebrates the rich diversity of the human experience, and expands the opportunities for writers and readers from within our community and its surrounding geographic region.

THE PUBLIC LIBRARY OF CHARLOTTE AND MECKLENBURG COUNTY

For more than a century, the Public Library of Charlotte and Mecklenburg County has provided essential community service and outreach to the citizens of the Charlotte area. Today, it is one of the premier libraries in the country— named "Library of the Year" and "Library of the Future" in the 1990s—with 23 branches, 1.6 million volumes, 20,000 videos and DVDs, 9,000 maps and 8,000 compact discs. The Library also sponsors a number of community-based programs, from the award-winning Novello Festival of Reading, a celebration that accentuates the fun of reading and learning, to branch programs for young people and adults.

This project received support from the North Carolina Arts Council, an agency funded by the State of North Carolina and the National Endowment for the Arts.